KT-369-452

RIEL
Novelization

by

Janet Rosenstock
and
Dennis Adair

Based on the original screenplay by Roy Moore

PaperJacks

Markham, Ontario, Canada

AN ORIGINAL CANADIAN

PaperJacks

One of a series of Canadian books
first published by PaperJacks Ltd.

RIEL

PaperJacks edition published March, 1979

This original PaperJacks edition is printed from brand-new plates
made from newly set, clear, easy-to-read type. No part of this
book may be reproduced or transmitted in any form or by any
means, electronic or mechanical, including photography, recording,
or any information storage or retrieval system, without permission
in writing from the publisher. PaperJacks editions are published
by PaperJacks Ltd., 330 Steelcase Road, Markham, Ontario
L3R 2M1.

ISBN 0-7701-0102-X
Copyright © 1979 by Janet Rosenstock, Dennis Adair
All rights reserved
Printed in Canada

RIEL

CONTENTS

Preface

This book does not claim to be history. Rather, it is fiction that employs historic figures. Some of the incidents described here did indeed happen, others did not, and still others had a reality far different from that recorded here.

The central character is of course Louis Riel, one of Canada's most controversial historic figures, a figure who could not have existed in any other time or place.

Many of the figures in *Riel* have been combined to form composite characters, just as real incidents often appear out of historic sequence. All conversations have been invented, and represent the collective imaginations of the combined authors.

What is real is the spirit of the history. Those years when Canada struggled against enormous odds to become a nation, when the United States posed a constant threat to Canadian western expansion and to the dream of uniting Canada from sea to sea, were among the most exciting years in Canadian history.

Louis Riel's life was dedicated to his people, the French-speaking Métis of the plains, and to the Indians, among whom the Métis lived for the most part in peace and brotherhood. He was also dedicated to his church, which at the time of this story was itself torn by conflicting ideologies, much as the church in Latin America is today torn between political action and the passive practice of religious rites. It is the age-old question—can the body be separated from the spirit?—and one which

Riel addressed himself to in both word and action. Can the Kingdom of Heaven alone be held out to the starving multitudes, or must the church heal the body before the spirit can be saved?

Louis Riel came down hard in answering this question and his answer brought innumerable forces into play. Two religious factions fought out their final battles, battles with origins in another land, at another time, on the great plains of Canada. In addition, two peoples re-enacted events on the Plains of Abraham for another generation, and again Canada's southern neighbour pushed for annexation.

Riel is a story of religious intrigue, cultural integrity, language rights, political indifference, and lastly, of human beings caught between two worlds. It is above all a story of dreams, conflicting desires played out on the great stage of continental expansion during a period of dramatic change.

One hundred years of Canadian history have failed to come to terms with Louis Riel, not because the man existed, but because the issues he clashed over with government still surround us. His dream is still far from a reality. *Riel* is dedicated to all historians, who know better than anyone that history is the greatest of all fictions.

1

Duck Lake: 1885

*Where's the coward that would not dare to
fight for such a land?*

Sir Walter Scott

"Where the hell are we?" James Howe addressed
himself to the volunteer trudging along next to him, his
Snider-Enfield slung casually over his shoulder.

"Somewhere near Duck Lake, must be a mile or so
to the post."

Howe was near the end of the ragged line, back with
the volunteers who had come from Prince Albert. They
were marching along in file, with the sleighs, Mounted
Police, and volunteers on horseback up front.

"Not used to snow in March," Howe grunted to his
companion. "Doesn't snow much in March in Ontario."

"Snows here," his companion responded. "Sometimes
right into April."

Howe was struck by the irony of the conversation.
Here they were, two strangers marching off after a
bunch of renegade Indians and Métis and calmly discussing the weather.

"How come you got no horse like the other Police-
men?" asked the volunteer.

Howe smiled. He wished he had a horse. Every bone
in his body ached.

"I just reported to Major Crozier and this detachment.
The horse I rode in on is pulling one of the sleighs."

"Where'd you come from?" The volunteer was not particularly interested in the answer to his question—it was just that talking took your mind off walking.

"Came in from Regina to Battleford and found the detachment had gone to Carlton."

"You had a long ride. Run into any trouble?" Howe suddenly felt stupid. He'd travelled across half the territory and still didn't know there *was* any trouble until he arrived at Battleford.

"Nope."

The volunteer seemed disappointed. Probably desperate to hear a good story to liven up the march.

"How many men are there?"

Howe had had neither the time nor the inclination to make a head count before they left. Now, in the falling snow, he couldn't count them anyway.

"Ninety some, I guess. You guys and forty-three of us." Howe felt secure in his training. There was a pride and power in his respected red uniform. He knew he himself was green and untested, but the volunteers—mostly farmers—were greener than he. Still, he didn't really know what was happening, or even why he was there.

"Tell me about the troubles here," said Howe. "I'm new out here. Only heard some rumours."

The volunteer hesitated. "Kinda hard to get the order straight." But he continued, "Really hard to say. There's this crazy Métis named Riel inciting some kind of an uprising. Then there's some Crees whooping it up and stealing guns from the Hudson's Bay posts." He paused and adjusted his rifle. "Heard this morning that a drunken savage named Wandering Spirit wiped out a bunch of people at the Frog Lake post. Don't know if that's true though, likely just a rumour. Them savages can't fight, least not like us."

Howe thought about this for a moment. "Are the Indians and Métis involved together?"

His companion shook his head. "Damn hard to tell,

son. Some Indians bringing white folks into Prince Albert for their own good, some Métis riding with us tonight. It's not the kind of thing where you can tell who's who."

Howe looked at the long file of men. It occurred to him that he probably wouldn't know a Métis if he met one, and he didn't much like the idea. He turned back to the volunteer. "It should be simpler than this—a man ought to be able to tell his friends from his enemies and the civilians from the rebels," he said flatly.

The volunteer laughed. "Friend, this is the West, and there ain't much hope of that. Out here you judge a man by how he carries his rifle. If he points it at you, he's an enemy."

Howe shook his head. "Hate to wait that long to find out."

"What's Major Crozier like?" Howe himself was confused by the man who had accepted his papers so abruptly and who now marched them through the darkness without explanation.

"A bastard!" came the reply. "And he don't like leading us volunteers. First he asks for us, then when he gets us, he acts like we're scum or something."

"I don't understand."

"Most of us don't like the half-breeds or the savages. Crozier, he likes some of them, got a lot of Métis friends. Told us to keep our damned opinions to ourselves."

Howe shrugged and peered into the darkness. The snow was falling more heavily now and visibility was very poor.

"That a cabin up there on the left?"

The volunteer stepped out of line for a second and craned his neck. "Sure looks like one. Probably deserted."

"Be nice to be inside in front of a fire," James Howe smiled.

"Be nice to be anywhere but here," the volunteer grumbled.

James Howe thought about a young woman, a fleeting vision of golden hair and a laughing face running across his memory. "Left a girl in Toronto, name of Ann Mason. She hopes to come West next summer."

"Pretty?" the volunteer asked. "Gonna get married, uh?"

James Howe smiled to himself. "I guess. She does the planning."

The volunteer laughed. It was a pleasant enough conversation for two would-be soldiers marching to fame and glory. This was the Saskatchewan country in March, 1885, and in less than ten minutes both men would be dead.

Major L. N. F. Crozier and Lawrence Burton, his lieutenant, rode side by side through the darkness ahead of the sleighs. The narrow, icy, pitted road from Fort Carlton to Duck Lake made the going rough, and the snow severely limited their vision.

"Someone's coming, sir." Burton pointed ahead at two horsemen riding hard. Crozier could barely see them in the distance. Suddenly they appeared like two white ghosts emerging from the night. Crozier held up his hand and the line of men and supplies came to an abrupt halt.

"It's MacKay and Conrad, sir." Crozier breathed a sigh of relief. Just the forward scouts coming back to report. Damned snow, he thought. Too wet and sticky. Take a warm fire to dry the men out tonight.

MacKay and Conrad reigned their horses in and moved abreast of the two men. Crozier saw the look of fear in their faces and instinctively looked beyond them into the darkness.

"Up ahead," MacKay gasped, breathless. "Métis— armed, a line of 'um."

Crozier barely waited for him to finish. "Get those sleighs across the road!" His voice bellowed through the darkness, and the black mass of men suddenly came alive. "Get in firing defence positions!"

Shouts reverberated from every direction as Burton directed the men and sleighs into a defensive line. He turned to one of the volunteers. "Get back down that line and get those men tight!" The man jumped with fright and then rushed away, passing the order as he ran down the line.

"There's two coming on their own." Conrad pointed off into the darkness. Crozier turned and squinted. The two solitary figures looked like moving snowmen. They halted about a hundred yards from the sleighs and waited. Crozier could see that one had his hand up, palm outward.

"MacKay, come here! Looks like they want to talk." MacKay galloped to Crozier's side. Andrew MacKay was an English Métis. He spoke little French but a lot of Cree.

"Stay with those sleighs, Lieutenant Burton! We're going out to see what's up."

Burton waved and watched as the two men pulled away and rode slowly toward the figures waiting silently in the blowing snow.

"Blessed be the peacemakers," muttered a man named Grenfield. He and Burton and another man were standing in front of the sleighs. The others, rifles poised, were crouched behind. The three men watched as the two Métis moved forward. Crozier and MacKay edged forward too.

"One's a Métis, the other's an Indian," said McVale. "See, you can just make out his feather." Burton nodded. He really didn't care what they were as long as they didn't end up fighting. He looked around him. The terrain was bad—they were on low ground and couldn't see a thing.

His eyes returned to the four men on horseback. They were talking now, close enough to touch each other.

A shot rang through the stillness. "What the hell?" McVale yelled out. The Métis, Burton thought, was down in the snow. MacKay fell next. Crozier was riding back at full speed, low in the saddle so no one could even see him. Shots rang out from all sides.

Privates McVale and Grenfield crawled behind the sleighs as Burton screamed, "Hold your fire!" He didn't want the idiots to kill their commanding officer, who was headed straight for the shelter of the sleighs.

"My God, what happened?" Burton looked into Grenfield's pale face. "I think the Indian tried to grab MacKay's gun. Couldn't really see that well."

Crozier skidded in behind the sleighs. He dismounted and slapped the rump of his horse, sending the animal into the nearby bush. He was breathless and in a foul temper.

"God damn!" he swore, over and over. Just what he didn't want! A fight in the middle of nowhere with a bunch of untrained, trigger-happy volunteers who would probably shoot themselves in their own feet. "God only knows how many sharpshooting Métis there are out there!" He said it to Burton, who was trying to find a target.

"I can hear where they're shooting from, but I can't see anything," replied Burton.

"They're all around us." Crozier pointed to the seemingly deserted cabin down the line and to the left. "Bunch in there too," he said flatly. He closed his eyes for a second. What a position! Colonel Irvine off to pick up reinforcements, him out here with forty-six trained men and a bunch of farmers. To top it all off, Fort Carlton was totally indefensible and his headquarters at Battleford not much better. A pile of muck it was. God damn! Those mucky-mucks in Ottawa had really done it this time!

Major Crozier bit his lip. He, an officer experienced in the ways of the Métis, had just walked into a bloody buffalo pen! He kicked the side of the sleigh and looked out along the line of inexperienced men. "Dear God," he muttered, "I don't want a massacre."

The Métis were indeed on all sides and bullets whizzed

through the air, ricocheted off rocks, and kicked up snow where they struck. Crozier saw that Burton had gotten the small cannon into position. It fired once, and then fell silent.

"What the hell's the matter with that thing?" Crozier yelled.

Burton looked back, distressed. "The gunner put the shell in before the powder, sir. It's out of commission!"

Crozier's anger grew. The nitwits were firing wildly at nothing and wasting ammunition. The cannon was useless. He looked back down the line and suddenly realized with horror that the volunteers were blindly charging the cabin. He ran down the line and seized one of the men who had stayed behind. "Who gave that goddamned order, soldier?" His raging voice could now be heard above the gunfire. It was filled with frustration.

"Fall back! Fall back!" he ordered. All around him men ran blindly, confused, helpless in the darkness, easy targets for the Métis snipers. The wounded who could be reached were thrown on sleighs.

Crozier moved forward, this time with the Police, to cover the retreat. He could see some of the Métis line now, and a lone rider dashing back and forth in front of his men, exhorting them on. Crozier blinked. It was Gabriel Dumont, one of the Métis leaders, riding low and giving directions. Even in the semi-darkness he was easily recognizable to his old friend.

Just then, Burton's shot rang out and Dumont fell from his horse. "Fall back!" Crozier's voice bellowed, but his eyes remained fixed ahead. Burton turned to move back. With a strange sense of relief, Crozier saw Dumont struggle to his feet and remount.

Another figure halfway up the rise was now visible. He appeared to be holding a huge cross at arm's length and his voice was deep and resonant as it travelled through the night ". . . In the name of God who created us . . . Courage, my brothers!"

A volunteer fired, but the figure was well out of

15

range. Crozier jerked the volunteer backward and sneered. "Stop wasting ammunition you greenhorn sonofabitch!" The volunteer was startled but did not reply.

Crozier raised his arm and again yelled, "Fall back!" This time all the men obeyed, and Crozier called for his horse and mounted. Now he ordered a headlong retreat into the darkness.

"Damn fools!" he muttered. Half the horses were dead—tied together and caught in the crossfire. He hadn't counted the dead or wounded yet. Most of them had fallen charging the cabin. Now the rebels had all the rifles from the Duck Lake post and some of his own as well. Eight horses captured, five of the seven sleighs in Métis hands. "Damn fools!" he repeated. He included himself in his curse. He knew he had walked right into a trap. The scouts had spotted the decoy line, but not the hidden sharpshooters. He looked around. Where the hell was that English half-breed, Conrad? He wondered if he could be trusted. Nice place to come to a halt—low ground and a cabin full of Métis sharpshooters. Probably led right into it, he thought. A fine muck pot! First the Métis and their new messiah, then the Indians, and now he wasn't sure if he could trust his own scout.

He comforted himself. At least they weren't being followed. He wondered how badly Dumont had been hit. Considering the condition of the column, he wondered . . . it didn't seem like Dumont, a sound military strategist, not to seize this kind of opportunity.

Burton rode up next to him. "Are we headed back to Carlton, sir?"

"No. Prince Albert." Burton did not look surprised. "That bad, sir?"

"That bad, Burton. We'll have to abandon Carlton and Battleford. They're indefensible without large numbers of reinforcements."

"Yes, sir. Do you think we'll have to make a stand at Prince Albert?"

Crozier shook his head. "God, I hope not. I'd hate to have to defend Prince Albert with this lot." He motioned back to the volunteers, most of whom had lost their horses and were now hightailing it for the town. No, Crozier said to himself, God save me from leading any more volunteers into combat!

2

Memories of Childhood: 1850s

You are, when all is done—just what you are.

Goethe

"Here, give me some help with this one!"

Guy Lefevre came over to Jean Tremblay and together they lifted the scarlet-clad body of the Policeman into the cabin.

"He's a big one!" said Lefevre, letting his half of the body down in front of the stone fireplace.

"All the redcoats are big ones," Jean answered wearily.

"He's young too. Looks like one of us got him right between the eyes." They both stood and looked at James Howe's body.

"Too bad he's so young. Looks like a nice *anglais*. Good face." Guy bent down and wiped the face, and some of Howe's blood came off on his fingers. He rubbed the blood curiously. "This pure blood?" he asked Jean.

"I guess." Jean leaned over and looked into the pale blue eyes. "Yeah, I think he's all *anglais* all right."

Guy stared at his fingers. "Looks like Métis blood. What's the difference between our blood and pure blood?"

Jean crossed himself three times. He did not like to have to look at bodies, nor did he enjoy killing. "We're half Indian, half French. We just talk about the blood, that's all. But it's not the blood, it's what's in the head."

Guy looked up at Jean. "Gabriel says half Indian, half French, the big winners!"

"We win and then we loose. Don't matter. Even when we're right we're wrong." Jean knew that Guy was young, too young to remember the Red River and much too young to remember the vast herds of buffalo.

"Hey, get his gun and holster. Better take the coat too. He won't be needing it now. We leave all the bodies here so the wolves won't eat them. Coupla days, Gabriel let Crozier come back and take them—soon as he knows that's all he's gonna take."

"Is Gabriel all right now?" Guy asked with concern.

"Yeah, he got hit in the head, hardest part of him. He was dizzy for a while, but he's all right now. C'mon now, Guy, we got to go back to Batoche. Everybody else is already gone."

Lefevre gathered up the rest of the things and the two men left the cabin.

"Too bad all the young ones have to die," Guy said.

"But you're young too," Jean answered.

Guy smiled. "Métis born old these days. I'll probably die soon too."

"I thought if I could read like Louis, I would be able to answer all the questions. I always had a lotta questions. Louis always had a lotta answers."

"He talks for us," Guy said. "He's different than us."

"The priests took him young. Said he was a smart one and taught him to read. Then they sent him away to school."

The two men mounted their horses and, riding slowly, headed back toward Batoche.

"No hurry, lot's of time," said Jean. He was thinking about Louis and about questions. Louis had found the answers in books. Reading must be important when a man has questions. He knew that answers were good to have—if they were the right answers.

Jean drifted back in time, back to the Red River settlement, back to when he and Louis were children. He should have paid more attention then, maybe he wouldn't have so many questions now. His first memories went back to about 1852, when he was eight or nine years old. Like so many Métis children, Jean's birth had not been recorded with the parish priest, so even now he did not really know exactly how old he was.

Fort Garry was a small place in the 1850s. At that time it was surrounded by a high wall with turrets in all four corners. It flew the Hudson's Bay flag because the Bay was the only government in the territory.

Inside the fort was the Bay trading post, some barracks, and only two or three houses. Outside were a number of Indian teepees, which were used by the Cree when they came to trade their furs. A little upstream and across the river, at the fork of the Red River and the Assiniboine, was the small community of St. Boniface. Here many of the Métis had built houses, where they lived between buffalo hunts, while some farmed the land to provide extra food. Smaller Métis communities could be found along the river to the south.

The Riel house was upstream, on the Seine, a small tributary of the Red. It was different from the other Métis houses in that it had a sense of permanency about it, and Jean liked to go there with Louis. He always imagined the Riel house was like the houses in Fort Garry. In any case, it was not like his own house with its sparse, rough furniture and its bareness.

Unlike the other Métis boys, Louis was usually studying with the priests. As children, Louis' studies limited their time together to occasional horseback rides together and rare visits to the Riel household. Jean remembered well one such day—it was the day Louis had explained "words."

"What are those?" Jean asked Louis. The two eight-year-olds had stopped at Louis' house for something to eat.

"They're words," replied Louis, indicating the sets of strange black characters on the page.

"You can read them?" Jean asked.

"Some." Gently taking the book from his hands, Louis turned it upside down (which Jean later learned was right side up). He knew Louis could read, but Louis had answered modestly because he was not a braggart.

"How can you read them? Where does one stop and the other begin? Tell me about the words."

Louis thought for a moment. Even as a child he had shown the makings of a teacher, but words were hard things to explain, even to a friend like Jean.

Characteristically, Louis put his hand over his mouth and frowned. Jean could see he was thinking, trying to find just the right way to explain "words." After a few minutes Louis' eyes brightened.

"How do our brothers the Cree call us?"

Jean did not know what this had to do with "words," but he answered anyway, confident that he did know the answer. "They call us Métis!"

Louis shook his head. "No, not that. How do they call us when they don't speak?"

"Oh!" Now Jean understood. He made the sign, fore-fingers of each hand circling each other, the extended finger of the right hand drawn down the front of the body from the right side of the head.

Louis smiled. " 'Wagon-man.' That's how the Cree call us. The sign describes a man in his wagon, a man always on the move going here and there."

Jean nodded, so Louis continued.

"The words are like a sign, each meaning something different." Louis was triumphant in his explanation. Jean was not sure he really understood Louis' answer, and anyway, he was tired of playing pupil—now he wanted to be the teacher.

"Come on," he urged, "let's get back to the horses, let's ride some more." Poor Louis, he didn't really like to ride, or shoot either.

Some time after his first visit to the Riel house, Jean had asked his father about the Riels. He asked why they were so different.

"All the Métis together have a tradition," Jean's father had told him. "But the Riels, they have a tradition all by themselves." After that there were many stories about the Riels, and Jean heard them all. Louis Riel the Elder was the acknowledged leader of all the Métis. He had been chosen leader for many reasons, not the least of which had to do with the woman he had married. Before Riel had taken her as his wife, she had been called Julie Lagimodière. She was the daughter of the first white woman in the Northwest, and the younger sister of the first white child born in the land of the "wagon-man" and the Cree.

Julie, like her famous sister Reine, was not Métis, but both were helped into the world by Cree women and raised among the Cree and the Métis. Their young mother, Marie Anne, was a legend, a white woman born in Maskinongé, who had accompanied her adventurous *coureur de bois* husband across half a continent to the Red River.

Louis' father had been born at Isle à la Crosse, a Hudson's Bay trading post in the Saskatchewan country. He was the son of a French Canadian and a Métisse mother (half French, half Montagnais). Thus, Riel the Elder was one-fourth Indian and young Louis was one-eighth. This was far less than most Métis, but blood was symbolic in the community where tradition and language were everything.

Most of the stories Jean's father told him about Riel the Elder had to do with the Hudson's Bay Company, which tried to rule the West with an iron hand. As Jean's father told it, it all began way back in the 1840s. The old Bay had wanted it all—the furs that the Indian and Métis brought in, and all the customers too. You got paid a little for your furs, and you paid a lot for the guns, knives, stoves, and pots you needed. Jean's father said he would have done the same, if he had been with the old Hudson's Bay.

If you sold to the Company, you had to buy from them too. Somehow you never sold for as much as you had to buy, and you always ended up owing their agent, McTavish, more money than you got. "Those old Bay traders," his father had said, "were old Scots or half-breeds who were half Scots, half Indian. They paid five shillings for a buffalo robe. But we soon found out where else we could go. Down in St. Paul, south of the border, we got two dollars and fifty cents for the same robe, and that bought more pots, stoves, tools, and whisky. The Yankee traders were tough, but they just got things cheaper to start. All the stuff the Métis wanted was made in the States. The Company, they imported from England and then brought their goods overland, so they were expensive. We would decide to buy some American whisky, and then be off, headed south along trails unknown to the Company agents. Smuggling just became a way of life . . . and why not? What's a damn border anyway? Métis don't need maps!"

Jean's father always paused here in his story. He always wanted to make sure Jean understood that like the Cree, the Métis went where they wanted, that the border was just an imaginary line, and that no one knew exactly where it was anyway. If you stood in one place you were in British North America, in the territory owned by the Hudson's Bay, if you stood in another, you were an American. The answer in those days to the question, "What are you?" depended on where you were at the time. Sometimes it was convenient to be one thing and sometimes another.

"The trouble in Red River started slowly when the old Company started losing money." Jean's father liked this story best. "We got told they owned the land, but they didn't send nobody to get us off. We were too many, some said more than five thousand Métis, and a lot of Cree. So the Company, it said, 'No more exporting south.' 'Exporting' they called it. They sent out agents and they say, 'If you sell in the south, in Pembina or St. Paul, you gotta pay a tax, and if you buy there and bring it back home, you gotta pay another tax.' It didn't work, 'cause we just took a wider cut across the prairie. There was too much prairie and not enough agents and we were too smart for them. Then, after a while, agents began searching Métis homes for contraband furs. They stopped the wagons and searched them too, and made new homeseekers sign an agreement not to import goods from Pembina or St. Paul and not to sell furs there. No agreement, no land."

Jean's father paused and grinned. "But we follow the buffalo and they don't know no border line, so we don't know no border line.' Jean could always remember the look of sweet reason on his father's face.

"That crazy Scot trader who ran the old Bay, McTavish, he jumped with rage. The smuggling increased and the Company, in retaliation, even began to censor the mails. Not that so many people wrote letters—it was just the idea of the thing. Even so, the letters just got to be one more thing that was smuggled . . . and more shillings for the Métis who ran the letters across the border.

"Then we had Louis' papa draw up a petition to the Hudson's Bay. We asked what our rights were. We got told we didn't have none. Old Riel, he wrote letters for us all the way to London, England. He just wrote and wrote. Well, when the government didn't answer any of our letters we whooped it up and McTavish got scared. Pretty soon an Imperial regiment came down and stayed with us and we had the martial law. Well, we were real quiet then, went on smuggling of course, but we were just real quiet for two years. 'Crazy like the French,' eh? Well, we had some of the Indian patience as well.

"The old Red River, she was quiet and peaceful and lovely. Her Majesty's troops just sat and sat. 'Bout the only thing they do is contribute to the English Métis population. We just all go about doing the normal things

24

and the commander, he thinks old McTavish is crazy and so they finally leave. As soon as they pull out, we begin again."

Now Jean's father was getting to the good part of the story.

"Guillaume Sayer was one of the three they finally caught. They brought him and two others to a trial. Well, we just damn well had enough! Enough of some dumb line you couldn't see, enough of waiting, enough of being told who to buy from and who to sell to. Riel, Louis' papa, he have enough too. He wrote enough letters to make his own book, but he didn't get enough back. So he told us, get the men, get the horses, get the guns. We all go to the courthouse in Fort Garry and surround it, maybe five hundred of us on horseback. McTavish, he turned white right up under that silly skirt he wears on Sundays. We tell them, 'You can try these men, okay, but you convict them, we gonna free them from the jail and free you from the trouble of breathing.' They go inside the courthouse and Louis' papa go with them. Then in a few minutes Louis' papa he come out and he come to the door all smiling and he shout, *'Le commerce est libre! Vive la liberté!'* Well, every crazy Métis on the prairie hear that shout!"

Jean loved the stories his father told him. Sometimes the details changed a little, but he understood that a story could be changed and still have truth. His father's story told the history of the Métis and of the Hudson's Bay Company, the beginning of a story Jean himself would often repeat to his own children.

Yes, it had all begun in the Red River, and when Louis came home it would begin again.

3

The Red River, 1868

*The explosion will not happen today. It is too
soon . . . or, too late.*

Frantz Fanon

As six pairs of dark eyes watched silently from behind
a small hill, a lone rider came over the crest of another
hill and, reaching the summit, stopped. The brooding
eyes saw that the man was not easy in the saddle.
Silhouetted against the sky, he was dressed in a dark
suit, but from the vantage point of the Métis watchers
they could not determine his age.

"Another lost *anglais*," said Elzéar Goulet without
surprise.

"For people lost, they sure find a hell of a lot,"
Gabriel Dumont added, not taking his gun sight off the
stranger. But Jean Tremblay knew he wouldn't shoot.
Dumont, he put everything in the sight of that Win-
chester, but he killed only buffalo when they were needed
for food. All the Métis were good shots, but Gabriel, he
was the best. He could hit any little thing you threw in
the air and hit it dead centre.

"Let's just watch the *anglais* a bit." Goulet was curi-
ous about this lone stranger. The *anglais* he knew never
rode alone.

On the hill, the rider's horse shifted restlessly as he
stood in his stirrups to stretch his weary muscles. His

dark brown eyes took in the scene below. How long? Ten years since he had seen that twisting, muddy red river moving off into eternity, the low rolling hills covered with tall prairie grass. He took a deep breath and smelled the clean air, alive with the aroma of sweet grass and the smell of dust picked up by the wind. A sharp bark-like call greeted him as a prairie dog popped out of its burrow, nose to the wind, standing on its hind legs and warning him to stay away from his hole. The rider sat back in his saddle feeling once again rooted and attached to the land of his boyhood.

He reached into his pocket and took out a small, worn, brown book and let it fall open as the wind decreed. Wherever God opened the page, there he would read: "The days of our years are threescore and ten; and if by reason of strength they be fourscore years, yet is our strength labour and sorrow, for it is soon cut off, and we fly away . . ."

The eyes looked up from the book and surveyed the scene below. Fourscore years . . . and one gone now! He heard the faint sound of the prairie owl and answered, "Not yet . . . not yet."

"What's he doing?" asked Goulet.

Dumont shrugged. "Just sitting."

"Probably trying to decide if he should stake out some land here. The *anglais* don't know that when it rains, everything runs downhill into the river." Tremblay laughed at his own joke.

The rider took up the reins again and began moving in the direction of a pile of rocks that formed a crude cairn. He knew the cairn held food, knew it had been placed there for Métis who might happen along, hungry. He bent his head, crossed himself, and offered a prayer for the pemmican cakes he was about to eat, before he began to remove the rocks.

"That *anglais*'s going to take our travelling food!" Goulet was angry. "You put something aside for the Métis and some damn *anglais* always comes and takes it.

Land, hay, women, food—*anglais* just help themselves and don't even say thank you."

"Not today," Gabriel shouted, and suddenly they were mounted, cresting the hill, and bearing down on the startled traveller.

As the man jumped up, a look of puzzlement crossed his face. Dressed in buckskin, some sporting colourful headbands, and all wearing leather moccasins, the ragged group charged at full gallop, a whooping shouting vision out of his past. The man dashed for his horse but it was too late—he was surrounded. Before he realized it he was on the ground, rolling in the dirt and wrestling, not at all playfully, with one of the unknown riders. He was a little taller than his assailants, but nowhere near as muscular.

"Why do you do this?" he shouted, and as a huge fist was about to come down upon him an absurd thought crossed his mind. His white, high collar was all filthy and his precious book had fallen from his back pocket.

But the fist stopped abruptly in mid-air and the dark angry face behind it suddenly broke into a wide grin.

"Riel? Louis Riel?" the man above him yelled in recognition. He was suddenly on his feet and being hugged. "Louis Riel! Friend of my childhood! Don't you know me? Elzéar. Elzéar Goulet!"

Dimly out of the past the faces of boys came to his mind . . . now the faces and bodies of men. Suddenly he realized he knew them all, except their apparent leader.

"This is no *anglais*," Goulet shouted, and they all gathered around. "This is Riel . . . he is Métis, one of us!"

As they rode along, the friends joked together and recalled their boyhood. Goulet slapped Louis on the back. "How could I have mistaken you for an *anglais*?" Tremblay smiled. "It is maybe the way he rides—so stiff, not like our brothers."

Louis grinned back. He had never been a good rider, and stiff was certainly how he felt. He had not been on a horse for ten years, and now he had been in the saddle for days.

"The horse goes one way and I go the other," said Louis good-naturedly. They all laughed, even Gabriel Dumont, who could hardly imagine a Métis who was not one with his horse.

This chance meeting with old friends filled Louis with warmth, and for the first time since he had left Montreal, he was happy. He felt it was an omen to have found these friends this way . . . to ride the last day toward home, not alone, but with Métis companions.

"You came back to help your mama?" asked Goulet, as they rode along. Louis nodded. They already knew his father had died. His father's name was known to all the Métis.

Hours later they set up camp just before the sun disappeared over the rise. In no time the fire was crackling noisily and they were reclining comfortably against the warm rocks in the fire's glow. Riel read his bible for a time in the flickering light, and finished his evening's prayer with three Our Fathers and three Hail Marys, his voice deep, resonant, powerful. The others were silent. "Hail Mary full of grace, the Lord is with thee, blessed art thou among women . . ." When he had finished, all except Dumont crossed themselves. He simply leaned against his saddle and listened, sometimes with his eyes open, sometimes with them closed.

"Been studying all this time, Louis?" Goulet asked. "You a priest now?"

Riel shook his head. "No, I left the seminary to study law."

"Good, good," said Dumont. "We need a lawyer more than a priest."

Riel smiled. "I'm afraid I'm not a lawyer either."

"Can you shoot, then?"

Riel looked down. "No."

"Good, good . . . not a priest or a lawyer and you can't shoot. Welcome to the Red River. You're just another Métis without a job . . . and without a gun you may end up hungry too.

"We're not farmers, we're hunters," Dumont said suddenly. "We get our food, shelter, clothes, songs, and even our dances, from the buffalo. We used to go every year from St. Boniface to Pembina. Everybody go, all at once. Nobody say, 'Go today,' 'Go tomorrow,' 'Go next week.' We just all go. Sometimes the first week in June, sometimes earlier, sometimes later.

"We get everything ready—the bows, arrows, and guns. The women, they get their things ready to clean the buffalo, sharpen all the knives good. The Bishop of St. Boniface, he appoints a priest to go on the hunt. Everybody come, Métis from everywhere. The *anglais* call it 'plains fever.' Then we make a big village and everybody choose their leaders. At night, a hundred fires in the great circle are burning and we dance and sing and make love.

"Then early in the morning we go out, all the leaders, and we decide on regulations. When everything is ready, we go out and we all find the buffalo. We chase them on horseback, we kill what we need, and the women come in and butcher and clean them. When you chase the buffalo you feel the wind and the sun. You pit yourself against a smart animal. You get killed if you're not careful.

"Too many Métis hungry now. Not so many buffalo. No land. Maybe we have to learn to farm, but we're not farmers.

"Welcome home to Louis Riel. Welcome back!"

Riel looked across the fire at Dumont . . . the latter's face was broken in a half-smile. Dumont caught Riel's eyes . . . large, dark, luminous, and strong. Who was this man who could hold the fearless Gabriel Dumont with his eyes, make him feel as though he were seen through, understood, penetrated. It made Dumont uncomfortable. He shifted against his saddle, then unexpectedly stood up, as if to move out of Riel's line of vision. He approached the fire.

"A test of strength anybody? Who takes on Dumont?"

To his surprise it was Riel who rose to join him next to the fire. They moved into position and quickly locked hands, as one of the men placed hot coals from the fire on either side of the two men. Dumont immediately pushed down and hard toward the red-hot coals, with Louis resisting. Their eyes were in constant contact; the force of strength, both physical and mental, was equal. Slowly, gradually, painfully, Dumont gained the upper hand and pushed Riel's arm into the bright coals. So great was his strain, Dumont did not realize he had won, but as the coals seared the cool flesh, Riel's expression never changed.

Dumont, in his own trance, suddenly realized what had happened. He jerked Riel's arm up and Tremblay and Goulet rushed over.

Riel looked at Dumont silently. "It's nothing . . . nothing." He brushed the others away, then wrapped a scarf around the large ugly burn and rolled over on his back. He was smiling at Dumont with the same broken half-smile he had seen on Dumont's face.

Dumont looked at Riel's smile and thought silently to himself, "He's either brave or a saint . . . or he's crazy." His guilt was eased, but only because Riel did not seem to be in any pain. In fact, he was still smiling . . . as though the triumph had been his!

Riel leaned back and closed his eyes against the flickering light. The smell of his own burning flesh had suddenly awakened something in him, an old dream, a forgotten reality. He couldn't be sure. But if it were a reality, why couldn't he remember more? The image drifted over the night air. Sometimes it came when he heard the *Kyrie eleison*, the call to prayer for mass, or saw a smooth cut stone, or a certain kind of candle. The feeling brought with it a rush of contradictory feelings, an almost primordial instinct to obey, to pray, to cleanse himself. Sometimes it would bring voices out of the past . . . but whose voices? Whose commands?

When he was alone, this distant memory of a dream frightened him. When he was with others he tried to pull his thoughts together, to remember more. Over the years this recurring nightmare—which he never remembered having dreamed—conjured up images of stone. Stone upon stone. A tomb? He didn't know. Somewhere in the darkness there was a single light, a candle flickering. Sometimes he heard low distant voices singing . . . the *Kyrie*? There was pain—the burning flesh? Hunger and weariness too. A voice said, "He should not be ordained." Another said, "It would be better if he were not . . ."

Louis shook his head. He knew it was a dream, an absurd dream. He had given up the seminary, had done it willingly. They had wanted him to continue; they had asked him to stay. It was a sign of guilt, this dream, his confessor had said.

Louis' arm did not pain him at all. Perhaps he was immune to pain from burns, he thought. He had a burn scar on his leg, but he had no memory of when or how he had obtained it. He crossed himself and pulled the blanket over his head.

The others were already sleeping. Only Gabriel Dumont continued to suck on his pipe and silently study the smoke that curled around his head and disappeared into the cool night air. The sound of night owls, crickets, and an occasional coyote howling to the distant moon comforted Louis. He wondered how he could have slept all those years without these sounds, God's sounds on the western prairie. His haunting dream had left him basking in the light of the stars that shone overhead.

Their patterns were clearly visible—the bear, the giant bird, the dog. He had always liked the bear, and strangely, he thought of Dumont with his long hair, beard, and broad shoulders. A rumbling, grumbling bear of a man, loyal, shrewd, and probably very kind. A little like his own father, Riel thought. Steady enough, but quick to the trigger. Dumont lacked discipline, he mused, but then perhaps he himself had too much discipline.

4

Macdonald's Plan for the West

*Conscience has no more to do with gallantry
than it has with politics.*

Richard Brinsley Sheridan

The House of Commons in Ottawa had just adjourned
its afternoon session and the spectators who had been in
the gallery were walking slowly down the great staircase.
Some had never been to Ottawa before, and they paused
to look at paintings that hung from the high walls.
Others were relatives of M.P.s—they visited the House
often and their passion was discussing the various debates
and personalities that dominated the government of
Canada. Ottawa was a small town, peopled largely by
politicians and civil servants; it was a town where gossip,
parties, and politics governed the lives of nearly everyone. People came to Ottawa to ask for something, or
they lived in Ottawa because they were somebody. Priv-
acy might have been an ideal, but it was never achieved.
What was not common knowledge was invented. Tongues
wagged on subjects ranging from the vital to the trivial,
and often it was hard to tell the difference.

Two matronly women swished their way down the
corridor in long taffeta dresses. The style of their clothing and their demeanor suggested they were both ladies
of means, Members of Parliament wives leaving the
gallery.

"And they talk about the *Mona Lisa*'s smile!" one said.

"Quite right," said the other. "Sir John certainly has a more puzzling smile."

"Yes," her companion agreed. "And what a time to be smiling."

"It isn't really a smile, more of a smirk."

"As if he always had a secret!" the other suggested. "Well, whatever causes it, it's simply withering if you ask me."

Donald Alexander Smith was walking just behind the two ladies, enjoying the snatches of conversation he picked up. He must speak to Sir John about his "simply withering" smile. Smith was a striking man with lively eyes, an engaging smile, and the longest beard on Parliament Hill. He was not an M.P., but he was close to Sir John A. Macdonald, the Prime Minister, and he had once been the head of the Hudson's Bay Company. Now, on his way to see the Prime Minister, he shared with him the dream of a railway west and was helping to find the money to make it possible. Not, he was daily discovering, an easy task.

Smith was an enigmatic man, not entirely sure that he liked politics. He had a way of pleasing people, of communicating with them, but he did not like to *have* to do it for political reasons. Business was something else—you made a decision, followed it through, took the consequences. Politics—and the longer he watched Sir John the better he knew—was not a question of "taking" the consequences, it was a question of making decisions that had no consequences. Small wonder so little was achieved over so long a period of time. Invariably verbiage was substituted for action.

The Prime Minister's office was large and panelled and had a characteristically high ceiling. The windows were huge and heavily draped in a dark brocade with lighter sheer ones letting in the sunlight. The Prime Minister's desk was a dark rich mahogany, clear of the papers and books one might have expected. An assortment of newspapers and other clutter was on a long table behind the desk.

"My work is nearby," the Prime Minister had once said, "but not always in front of me." It struck Smith that this rather neatly summed up the Prime Minister—a genuine distaste for what was behind him, and an anxiety about what lay ahead.

Sir John A. Macdonald's face was a craggy if benevolent one. His busy brown hair looked like clumps of unruly bushes sprouting from bare cliffs. He was a lean man, with dark eyes, and—the silly women in the hall had been right—an enigmatic smile.

The map of the new Confederation of Canada on the wall told of Sir John's ambitions and dreams. The provinces already in Confederation were marked in green. The remaining land, stretching from Ontario to the Pacific Ocean, waited to be taken, to be pencilled in and named. Sir John's vision was one of Canada from sea to sea. The hows, whys, and wherefores were not his concern. Sir John saw only the total. It was—and he never hid it—his destiny. He would have his dream, and even Smith knew that he would have it by hook, by crook, or by force. One way or another, British North America would become one of the biggest countries on earth. "A presence," he used to say, "must be established."

Today, Sir John was in the best of moods, smile and all. Preparations were complete and another gigantic piece of the map would soon be added. The Hudson's Bay Company had finally agreed to sell their vast territories to the government. Soon this territory, known as Rupert's Land, would be a part of Canada, with its own territorial government. Not for a few months yet, but the preparations were well under way. Sir John's green pencil was itching to colour in a new piece on the map.

Donald Smith cleared his throat. "McDougall's on his way up, Sir John."

"You don't like him do you, Donald?" It was a rhetorical question.

"No," Smith answered honestly "I don't, and you know it." Smith did not care how the Prime Minister himself felt about McDougall. He always made a point of saying what was on his mind, whether it was to God, the Prime Minister, or to anybody else.

"He's pompous, not overly bright, and he's wrong for the territory and the people who live there." There was that damn smile.

Sir John leaned back and looked at his friend. "I imagine there are some who like him . . . in Ontario in any case."

"He won't be governing Ontario, Sir John. Nor will he be governing Ontarians."

"There are settlers in the territory from Ontario."

"Few," said Smith. "Too few, I'm afraid."

"Now Donald, don't lose your perspective. He arranged for the Company to sell us the territory . . ." Smith wanted to interrupt, but he knew enough to hold his tongue. "If McDougall thinks being governor out there is his just reward, who are we to disagree?" Sir John had finished for the moment. A political animal at all times, thought Smith. How many Conservative votes could McDougall deliver? And would the trouble he might cause be worth it? The Prime Minister's eyes were still on him. Sir John A. Macdonald rarely took advice, but he often openly solicited it. Now Smith smiled at Sir John.

"Take care, my friend, that you see more than just the missing link to the West."

"Oh Donald . . . if that land were anything more than flat plains that boil the Indians in summer and freeze them in winter, do you think the Bay Company would agree to give it up? You must know how the Company thinks! For God's sake, man, you were once the head of it!"

"They wanted it for the furs, Sir John, it's not as

lucrative as it was. Times change, needs change. You want it for a railroad, for Canada!" Smith spoke evenly now. It was a point he badly wanted to make Sir John understand. "It's a third of a million square miles of prime real estate! Oh, you'll have it, Sir John, but it will be quite another thing to hold it. The French half-breeds don't understand the English, the English ignore the French, and the Americans have been eyeing all of it since . . ."

"Oh now Donald, the Americans eye everything that isn't nailed down. Are you saying I need a stronger man out there—one who can nail things down?"

Smith looked at Sir John. "Yes," he replied evenly. "Could be you need a stronger man."

The Prime Minister rubbed his chin, knowing full well Smith's plans and ambitions. "Priorities, my friend. I need you to finish financing the railway that will tie this country together. After that we can talk about your sugarplum dreams for that prime real estate. There's country enough . . . *when* it's tied together."

Smith took a deep breath. No more arguments, he thought. He had made his point and knew it was useless to continue in that vain.

A knock on the door interrupted his brief respite. They had both been so busy discussing William Mc-Dougall that they had forgotten he was about to arrive.

The door opened. "Mr. Prime Minister . . ."

The man coming through the door had thick jowls and was decidedly overweight. Smith fully expected him to sink to his knees and lick the Prime Minister's shoes. It had been Smith's experience that those who looked up to some men invariably looked down on others. Better, he thought, to look everyone straight in the eye.

"Ah, Mr. McDougall. You know Donald Smith, of course. Well, you'll soon be heading west now."

This, Smith could tell, was not going to be an important meeting of minds. There was something terribly ironic about it all. Here was the wiley Sir John A.

Macdonald, whose greatest dream was to unify Canada and join it from sea to sea, and that blithering idiot McDougall, discussing his forthcoming journey west via the United States (damn near the only way to get there, unless you had a lot of fortitude) and what he planned to buy when he stopped off in St. Paul. He wondered if the Yankees sold American flags for the Canadians to plant on territory they could only reach via the United States. Probably. They'd been selling everything else for years. In his heart Smith knew this was really Canada's biggest dilemma. The railroad, Sir John's persistent vision, might help, but he wasn't sure it was going to solve the problem of geography entirely.

He remembered reading some reports from Anthony Trollope, the British novelist and onetime journalist. Trollope had been travelling in Canada and the United States, in St. Paul and the Red River country, in 1861. He knew the Americans coveted the territory that lay to the north but did not believe invasion would be the method of acquiring it. Trollope had concluded that dependence on Yankee transport facilities and Yankee business enterprise might be the thing that would eventually do British North America in. Why invade a country, he reasoned, when you could end up buying it?

The Métis traded constantly with the Yankees. Some of his compatriots had even heard that they were trying to persuade the Métis to join the United States! That, he thought, would put a very big hole indeed in Sir John's map. No, McDougall was not the right man. In Smith's opinion he was worse than that—he was *exactly the wrong man*. A man who couldn't bring the Métis firmly into Canada, a man who might drive them in the end into the hands and hearts of the waiting Yankees, a man who knew nothing about the Fenians (Irish Republicans who constantly urged their Catholic Métis friends to turn South). Moreover, he was a simpering easterner who would spout and bluster if he couldn't have a hot bath. Damn. Why couldn't Sir John understand that this decision could have consequences—dire ones for Canada.

Smith was very weary. A lot of good it would do Sir John to get the money and build the railway if he lost the ground he was going to build it on. The country must, of course, be united, and the railway was part of it—an important part. Long-term goals, short-term necessities. Donald Smith was afraid they were going after one and ignoring the other.

5

Red River Revisited

Do your duty, and leave the rest to the gods.

Horace

"Hey there, Louis," Elzéar Goulet called out. "You almost home now. You glad?"

"I'm very happy, Elzéar, my brother," Riel called back. "Glad to be almost home, glad to have you ride this far with me."

"I'm going now, Louis. I come back when you settled in. We talk some more then, eh?"

He had already spurred his horse and was off at a gallop. The others had left earlier, when the sun was barely over the rise.

Riel rode slowly on, alone with his thoughts now. He wanted to be home, but he had a strange premonition about it. Riding along for the last hour he had been thinking about the seminary. Funny, when he was at the seminary he had always thought about home.

Life in the Red River settlement seemed to have stood still since he had left. Bishop Bourget of Montreal had asked him to keep in touch, had taken special care to stress over and over again that he, Louis Riel, would play a major role in events to come. And before he left Montreal, Father Charles McWilliams, his closest friend in the seminary, had sought him out and repeated the Bishop's concern. Yes, Riel thought, Bishop Bourget was right—the Métis way of life and the Catholic church were in danger in the Red River. The English settlers were growing in number and many of them were Orangemen from Upper Canada. They had brought with them their terrible prejudices, bred when they fought the Irish and the French and transferred whole to the French Métis on the prairies.

Not all the English were alike, of course. Some English farmers had been on the prairie since Louis' boyhood, some even resisted the tide of Canadian expansion westward.

Riel's eyes swept the scene before him, over the vast expanse of land that seemed to stretch forever in all directions. Surely there was room for everyone, surely accommodation could be made. This land belonged to no one, but it was occupied by the Métis, and occupation, Riel had learned, was nine-tenths of the law. Perhaps it was everything in the West, where the Métis, Cree, Sioux, Assiniboine, and even some of the English, had cast their lots together. In spite of the Bishop's warning of the Prime Minister's plan to establish a Protestant Confederation that would obliterate French culture and language in the West, the land and its people seemed peaceful enough. It was as it had always been. Time seemed to have left the prairie unchanged.

Riel slowed as he approached the small cemetery. The sight of the randomly placed crosses filled him with sadness. The one-room prairie church with its steeple raised heavenward had guarded the lonely graves of his ancestors for as long as he could remember. He had come or had been brought to this place often as a child. His mother had walked with him among the simple crosses and together they had recited the long and illustrious history of the Riels. On Sundays, he remembered, the bells of the little prairie church rang out, calling the Métis to mass, and voices raised in worship mingled with the souls of the departed.

Riel dismounted and tied his horse to the gate. He took the bible from his back pocket and the flowers he had collected earlier and approached the rows of crosses. Riel had last seen his father ten years before, but even prior to his leaving for Montreal, his father had been away much of the time. Louis could conjure up many faces from his boyhood, but for some unexplained reason the face of his father always remained featureless. It was substance without form. He had wanted to be nurtured in the shadow of his father's protection, he had craved above everything else the affection of this vision from his childhood. Louis Riel the Younger had never really known Louis Riel the Elder—the doer of all things, the legendary leader of the Métis.

Riel placed the flowers on the grave, opened his book, and began to read from the Psalms of David . . . David, the king of his people.

". . . Yea though I walk through the valley of the shadow of death, I will fear no evil: for thou *art* with me; thy rod and thy staff they comfort me . . ."

Louis Riel was thirteen and standing alone in this same cemetery when he turned to see the hideous, pock-marked face of the Dreamer.

"You come to talk with the spirit. You should come to listen," said Assywin.

"I do listen," the boy responded timidly. He was not afraid of the old Indian but he was uneasy. He looked into the Dreamer's face. He had seen the ravages of the disease before, and it had always troubled him. His mother had told him about the smallpox epidemic, how the infected Indians had shrieked and screamed in the night. They had gone in agony to their medicine men, but there was no medicine for this curse from the white man. In thirty thousand years of their history in that place, the Indians had never seen the devil of this disease before. Its ravages were greater than the white man's guns, greater than his lust for land, greater than the disease he gave their women when he slept with them. In their collective agony, with the sores of their coming death pouring forth with pus, they ran to the forts of the white men and to their houses. In the night they rubbed themselves against the walls and tried to give the illness back to those who had brought it.

The Dreamer was a survivor, but his eyes held the memory of his people's suffering. His spirit was infected with hatred, as his body had once been infected with smallpox.

"The ghosts of our warriors will rise up. They will join us in the final battle. The dead will return to fight, to take back our land."

The boy listened. He knew little of the Dreamers and their ghost dances. The old Indian told him the story of the white dog, of the ghosts, and he foretold the future.

"What do the spirits say?" Louis asked.

"We will fight together, we will win together—the Indian and the Métis. The spirit of our great warriors will return, the spirit of the Métis warriors will return. We will smoke together and do battle together."

Louis returned to his prayers, even as the thoughts of his encounter with the Dreamer faded. "I lift up my voice unto the Lord . . ." He wondered how in practice the Dreamer's faith differed from his own. Were not all the saints, angels, and the spirits of the righteous to be united in the Kingdom of Heaven when the final judgment came? Were not old warriors reborn? God in his wisdom has selected you, Louis Riel, you David, king, to be the salvation of your people.

"He was always an example to follow, Louis."

The voice startled Riel. He thought he was alone with his father and his memory of the Dreamer. He looked up into the bright, inquisitive eyes of Father Ritchot, the ruddy-faced priest who had confirmed him. Riel crossed himself and rose to meet the priest.

Father Ritchot continued. "He always looked for the truth. Always a good and loyal friend . . . stubborn though. He fought the Company. He was a restless man."

44

"People didn't always understand him." The phrase rang hollow in his ears, for Louis himself did not understand his father.

"The English, the Company . . . they still don't understand us. Nor I them. I only know there are more and more of them here every day."

Father Ritchot was a good man. He felt his flock endangered by these anti-Catholic English. Sometimes, isolated as he was, he felt he was the lone voice of a dying people, a shepherd whose flock was dispersing.

Louis felt the extent of Father Ritchot's pain. His face revealed the depth of his feeling, of his responsibility.

"Perhaps the English can be made to understand," Louis suggested. "The land is big enough. It is our faith that is small."

"Perhaps." The priest spoke without conviction. "Your father would have liked you to become a priest."

Louis smiled. "Bishop Bourget tells me one doesn't have to wear a cassock to serve God."

"Quite so, Louis, quite so. You are fortunate that the Bishop has offered you his counsel. He is a busy man, not many seminarians have the benefit of personal discussions with Bishop Bourget."

Louis knew that Father Ritchot was right. Indeed, he had always wondered about the Bishop's interest in him. From the very beginning he had showed his kindness, even in little ways. When he decided to leave the seminary, the Bishop appeared undisturbed. He spoke to him of the ways one could serve God, of how Louis could go home and with his education and his faith help the Métis find their voice and their will.

"What will you do now, Louis?"

Louis thought for a moment. Time, he had been told, would pass and he would be directed by circumstances, by prayer, by God.

"I'll help my mother first," he replied. "She wrote to me, asked me to come home. The farm needs work, there are fences to mend. My hands shall not be idle."

"And then . . ."

"Time will tell, Father, time will tell," Louis answered. "It was just time to come home."

The land here in the Red River was divided, as it was in Quebec. Each of the farms spread out from the river and shared mutual haying privileges. The Canadians divided land differently, into plots joined by roads. They shared very little with their neighbours; in fact, they seemed to build as far from one another as possible. Riel smiled to himself. What a people these English. They can't even stand each other.

It was natural for the Métis to build as the French in Quebec had built . . . practical too. The houses were not far apart, the farming was good, and the people had a community. And, they had protection. When the Métis had first come to the Red River, there were problems with some of the Indians. Not the Cree, but the Blackfeet and their wandering cousins the Sioux. Far-flung farms were indefensible but the English built them anyway. The Métis could defend their farms and the Indians soon came to respect their cousins, who were neither French nor Indian, but who were something of both.

Now the prairie wind was coming up. The winds that started their life in each of the four corners of the earth and blew gently, gathering strength as they rolled across the flatland, moved through the gentle slopes and valleys, prepared to struggle with the walls of the great mountain masses to the west.

The tall grasses blew in great soft waves as Louis Riel looked down on his family's homestead. The fences were collapsing, the paint was peeling and leaving the wood at the mercy of the elements, and the land was for the most part overgrown with scrub brush.

"The Métis," his father had once said, "were not meant to be farmers. We go where the wind goes, we follow the buffalo."

46

The door of the Riel home opened and a woman stepped out. She was smaller than he remembered, and thinner now than when he had left. Her long dark hair was in braids. The once thick black hair that revealed some distant Spanish ancestor was now streaked with grey. The colourful, embroidered dress she had worn when he left had been replaced by the black of her mourning. A silver cross hung heavily from the frail neck.

Julie Lagimodière Riel looked like a Métis in the distance, but on close examination, the slender waist, the smaller bones, the large grey eyes, and the delicate facial features betrayed her heritage. A speaker of Cree and of French, she shared the two cultures—the deep faith of her Catholic forebears and the mysticism of the Indian. "Bless me Father, for I have sinned." With those words the rosary fell from her hands. "Louis? Louis!" Her voice trailed off as she threw herself delirious with joy into his arms.

"It's all right, mother. I've come home . . . I've come home."

6

The Right to a Future

*Property is in its nature, timid and seeks protection,
and nothing is more gratifying to government than
to become a protector.*

John C. Calhoun

A stranger looking out at the long, winding lazy river,
at the peaceful farms and villages, or even at the community of Fort Garry itself, would never have guessed
that the seemingly peaceful settlements were seething
with unrest.

The vast majority of the people who inhabited the
Red River were Métis, who spoke French and who
practised Catholicism. Some said they numbered ten
thousand in the area, with many thousands more in the
territory. There were also many English half-breeds.
Some were sympathetic to the cause of the French Métis,
others were not.

The English settlers were also numerous, but few
subscribed to any specific political party and many
feared they might loose their land should any sudden
change in the status of the territory take place. A few
Americans had also settled in the great valley of the
Red River, and not surprisingly, they favoured annexation by the United States.

The Canadian settlers were so called because they
belonged to a specific political group called Canada First,
and thus they were differentiated from the other, gener-

ally apathetic English-speaking settlers. The leaders of the Canada Firsters were primarily of Orange sentiment from Ontario and were deeply resentful of the French Métis and the many Irish Catholics who had also come to live in the Red River Valley.

Dr. John Schultz, his outspoken wife, Elizabeth, Tom Scott, and Charles Mair were the leaders of the Canada Firsters. They demanded unity with Canada, and because they had influence in Ottawa, they knew much about the government's plans, enough to know that land staked out now would be far more valuable in the future.

It was Tom Scott's desire to show Elizabeth Schultz the land he had been surveying that brought them to the countryside this fine summer day. Now they were sitting together, breathless, beneath a low willow tree at the water's edge. In Dr. Schultz's absence they had become lovers, and now they were resting after a furtive coupling in the tall grass.

"This is my land now," Scott sighed easily. Elizabeth Schultz nodded her head. "It's a fine piece of property, Tom. It'll make you rich."

"I'll soon have more, much more." He rolled over on his back and looked up into Elizabeth's face. "And when the Hudson's Bay sells out to the government of Canada and the railway comes through, I'll be one of the biggest landowners in the territory. What do you hear from your 'dear' husband? What has he found out in Ottawa?"

"Nothing definite . . . yet." She paused. "It'll happen, of course. Our party has a great deal of influence in Ottawa. The Prime Minister is depending on us to make this territory Canada's. My husband will see to it—he's a man of influence."

"Oh yes, yes I know," Scott replied. "Otherwise, you would not have married him."

Mrs. Schultz leaned down and looked into Scott's eyes. "He won't be home for some time. He's busy making us rich."

Scott smiled and slipped his hand into her bodice. Her facial expression changed as the colour flowed into her cheeks. Nestling closer, she lay down beside him on the sweet-smelling grass.

As he undressed her, he said, "Let's have a little party on my new land, what do you say?"

In the distance, behind two great rocks, Gabriel Dumont and old Moiese Ouellette stood watching the scene below. Gabriel spit and then idly rubbed it into the earth with his foot. He did not like the foul-mouthed Scott, who was known even to the English as a bully and an ill-tempered braggart. This "man of property" was an uneducated labourer and surveyor, who ran whisky to the Indians for a living.

Dumont put his gun down. Even though he hated Scott, at the moment he was amused at the two lovers. He wondered what Dr. Schultz would do if he saw his young wife and his friend, Tom Scott, now. He himself might have moved off and left them to it, but old Ouellette was obviously enjoying the spectacle. Instead of leaving, they leaned against the rock and watched.

"How far you suppose that Scott can run with his pants down?" Ouellette asked.

Dumont shook his head. "First they sell whisky to the Cree, then they buy land from them. Now like two prairie dogs they crawl into their hole and *fourrent! Maudits anglais!*"

Ouellette smiled at Dumont's comments, knowing it was better not to laugh, since the wind was blowing in the wrong direction and they might be overheard. "She's got a good ass," he offered.

Dumont looked at him, a long, funny look. "You got good eyes for an old man of seventy-nine."

Not good enough, Ouellette thought. He would like to have been closer.

"C'mon," Dumont signalled. "A Métis won't learn anything from those two." Ouellette followed, glancing over his shoulder once before they reached the horses.

Dumont's thoughts returned to Scott. Something was up, something he did not yet understand, but something important. How was it that the Métis could not get land rights from the Hudson's Bay Company, but these "Canadians" were already staking out property, property that was not even theirs?

Ouellette watched Dumont as they rode along. He knew without asking what his old friend was thinking. Gabriel Dumont was now the acknowledged leader of the Métis. He had led them often on the hunt and nearly always acted as a "free rifle," giving his kill to the old, the sick, or those women who were without men. He was known for his quick wit and ready smile. Gabriel was tough, but he stood straight as an arrow and in battle was utterly ruthless. His heart, it was said, was as big as the land he rode through. He could give himself totally to someone or something, or hold back completely. Those who fell under his protective wing were there forever, regardless of what they did or how they behaved. All of Gabriel's decisions were final, for he was a man who could deal with consequences. Ouellette knew that Gabriel could never farm, could never settle down, could never be a man of property. He also knew that Gabriel was worried, not for himself, but for the Métis. Farmers they were not, but now survival might depend on tilling and working the land.

"And what did our friend Riel find out in Fort Garry? Did he find out from McTavish if the Company would give us deeds to our property?" asked Dumont.

Ouellette shook his head. "We go there now, Gabriel. Riel has a paper to read us, to explain . . . it's why he has sent the message to come."

"Paper!" Gabriel spit on the ground again. "*Anglais* and their paper! *Merde*. They go around putting stakes in the ground and then they say, 'Where the stakes are, this is our property!' We get nothing but paper! And it's not a deed, it's paper saying why we can't have a deed."

Until recently, Dumont had never really cared about having a deed to the land on which his house was built. As far as he was concerned, the land was where you came between hunts, it was where Madeleine, his wife, grew a few vegetables. Still, deep in his heart he could see what was happening. The buffalo were disappearing. They got fewer and fewer every year. Young Métis would have to learn to farm, because the buffalo would not last forever, in spite of all the precautions that had been taken. The Métis had drawn up a paper, a set of rules for hunting, and before the hunt the rules were communicated to the great camp by crier:

No buffalo run on the Sabbath Day.

No party to fork off, lag, or go before without permission.

No person or party to run buffalo before the general order.

Every captain with his men in turn to patrol camp and keep guard.

For the first trespass against these laws, offender to have his saddle and bridle cut up.

For the second trespass against these laws, coat to be taken off offender's back and be cut up.

For the third offence, offender to be flogged.

Any person convicted of theft—even to the value of a sinew—to be brought to the middle of the camp, and the crier to call out his or her name three times, adding the word "thief" each time.

Well, a man knew he was helpless without his saddle and his bridle, and he would freeze without his coat. The Métis all obeyed because the law of the hunt had been made by them all, for them all. Thus were wasteful methods of hunting the buffalo outlawed. The Métis and Indians took what they needed, but they were careful not to take more and never to kill the young calves. However, the buffalo were now being killed commercially, and Dumont feared in his heart that one day, like the Indian confined to a reserve, the buffalo would also be confined, the last survivors of a dead species. Land to farm when the buffalo were gone was now important to the Métis nation.

Now, as the two men approached the Riel homestead and saw Louis standing near the door, Ouellette pointed to the newly painted and repaired fence. "It looks better now. Cleared some of the land too," he added.

Dumont surveyed the homestead. Louis did seem to have done quite a bit around the place.

"Good thing he come home. His mama, she need someone," Ouellette added.

Louis saw them coming in the distance. Old Ouellette and Dumont made a strange pair, he thought. He and the others, Jean, Goulet, all of them had had meetings since he returned. Dumont always asked about his arm, but unlike the others, never asked Louis to read anything for him, or to write either for that matter. Between them there was a grudging respect, even the beginning of a friendship. He knew that his father and Gabriel's had been friends, but the two boys had not known each other as children because old Isidore, Gabriel's father, had moved his family away for a time and did not return until after Louis had gone to Montreal to study. Louis knew enough of Gabriel Dumont to know that one had to win his respect—he knew he was being looked over and that Gabriel was slow to make judgments.

A few days earlier they had asked Riel to go to Fort Garry and speak on behalf of the Métis with old McTavish, who still ran the Hudson's Bay post. The Métis had all heard rumours, all had had promises made to them, but now no more was being said. So Louis had gone, and now he knew that the rumours were true, that Bishop Bourget had been right, and that the uneasiness of Father Ritchot was not unjustified.

Fort Garry was bigger now than when he had left. More houses, some quite elegant for the prairie, now filled the streets of the expanded fort. Farms could be seen stretching out westward, and to the south and north. The fort even had a small hotel, and it did not

53

surprise Louis that Fort Garry now had visitors as well as settlers, and that it was full of Canadians. The Hudson's Bay Company, however, looked exactly the same, and the flag that he and his friends had grown up under still fluttered in the breeze.

He remembered his visit to the post. Inside, old McTavish sat behind the same cluttered oak desk. Louis was wearing his stiffly starched white shirt, his dark suit, and his moccasins. McTavish looked into his pale face and dark eyes.

Louis was direct. "My friends are asking me about deeds to the land they live on, Mr. McTavish. Or even the land where they live between buffalo hunts."

McTavish eyed him like an older fox protecting its young. He had known Louis as a boy and he remembered his father well.

"The buffalo are disappearing, aren't they?" McTavish half smiled and then nodded. "But who knows that better than the Métis, eh?"

Louis did not shift his gaze. That wily old Scotsman, he thought to himself, would steal a man's coat in midwinter and sell it back to him for a good profit.

Louis stuck to the point. "What about the land rights?"

McTavish rubbed his chin. "Top of the list for the new governor when he takes over next month."

Louis did not get another chance to speak, for Elizabeth Schultz breezed into the office. McTavish was up out of the chair and grasping her gloved hand.

"Mrs. Schultz! This *is* a surprise! What do you hear from the good doctor?" Mrs. Schultz's gaze went beyond McTavish and settled on Louis. She took him in, head to toe, in one perfunctory glance. Her eyes stopped on the moccasins. She turned warmly to McTavish.

"Oh, he writes me the new governor is fond of champagne. I'll need enough for two hundred people. A little reception you know."

Louis felt uneasy with this woman. She had barely acknowledged his existence and without a word had discarded him. He had seen some of these English "ladies" in Montreal. John Schultz, "the good doctor," had obviously married his match. Riel reasoned she must be at least twenty years his junior, and it was not difficult to tell that life in Fort Garry had not been what Mrs. Schultz had had in mind.

"We've already printed newspaper announcements," she continued. She handed McTavish the folded paper and looked once again in Louis' direction.

McTavish turned, suddenly remembering Louis was there. "Young Louis Riel is back from Montreal for a visit."

"Perhaps you can read the announcement to your friends then. Do you read English?" she asked Riel.

He met her question and her eyes. He was sure his face expressed his feeling toward her. *"Oui, Madame Schultz, je lis anglais."*

"Good!" she replied, turning abruptly back to McTavish. "I must be going now, dear Mr. McTavish, and you won't forget my champagne, will you?"

Later, Louis read the paper. He read it now to Ouellette and Dumont and the others who had arrived before them: "The wise and prudent will be prepared to receive and benefit by the changes to be made when Canada assumes sovereignty, whilst the indolent and careless, like the native tribes of the country, will fall back before the march of superior intelligence . . ."

Louis put the paper down. "We must write a—" Dumont cocked his rifle and stood leaning against the fireplace. The sound of a rifle being cocked always brought immediate attention. Louis did not finish his sentence.

"We going to fight fire with paper?" Dumont asked in a suppressed rage. Everyone's eyes were on him. Louis was sitting, Dumont standing across the room. Louis cleared his throat, but his voice was equal to Gabriel's.

"We fight paper with paper . . . and fire with fire. For now, the Canadians fight with paper."

There was silence. He knew he had chosen the right words.

"They can't take over. Their government has no jurisdiction. We have alternatives, choices. We can set up a provisional government. Under the law of nations we will be correct; they will have no alternative but to listen!"

He finished and drew a breath. Dumont said nothing.

"Let us elect a committee and form a council for a provisional government." There was nodded agreement. "Go out to the districts," he continued, "have each of them send a representative. We can fight them with their own laws." It was agreed.

Louis closed his eyes. There was shuffling and talking, argument and agreement. The meeting place was arranged, the Métis were to be notified.

"First your way, and then mine," Dumont said.

"No," Ouellette interrupted. "You lead together. One of you is not enough. You, Louis Riel, are to be the head; you, Gabriel Dumont, the heart."

More argument, more talk. It was the way of the Métis, a unique but workable democracy. Finally, it was agreed, and Dumont and Riel had embraced like brothers. In that moment their two spirits met. Gabriel Dumont took Louis Riel into his protected circle of blood brothers, and Louis Riel had found equality with the father he had never really known.

Later, riding through the night on that, the first of many anxious rides, Dumont found himself repeating the phrase from the English paper. ". . . fall back before the march of superior intelligence . . ." Superior, *merde*! He thought of Riel with pride. The Métis would show the *anglais* what intelligence was!

It was a few days after the Métis meeting and no one was there when it happened. If they had been, Tom Scott might well have got a bullet between the eyes.

Young Napoleon Nault was barely sixteen, a shy, slightly built boy with light hair and dark eyes. Unlike many Métis, Napoleon enjoyed farming. It pleased him to watch the seeds he planted grow into healthy, thriving plants. He took pride in the fact that the Nault homestead was one of the most developed, for he tilled the land lovingly and it rewarded his care in bountiful harvests.

The surveyors numbered four in all. Tom Scott was one of them. They said they were surveying for the new road, but Napoleon protested.

"This is Métis land," he said. "This is where we keep our hay."

Scott walked forward. He was a tall man, and well built. Some said he had been a professional boxer once. Napoleon had always thought the man cruel and hateful.

"Boy, this is government business. Good for you. A road right past your farm."

Napoleon looked the larger man in the face. "No, you're surveying in the middle of the farm!"

Scott laughed and spit. "Middle, huh? Doesn't really make a damn bit of difference does it, half-breed. You ain't got no deed. You ain't got nothing!"

Napoleon was angry. He turned from Scott in a rage. He had tears in his eyes and he did not want Scott or the others to see them. He grabbed some of the surveyors' equipment and threw it into their wagon.

"Get out of here!" he shouted.

One of the men said, "Maybe we'd better wait . . ."

"No half-breed's gonna be rude to me!" Scott blustered, grabbing Napoleon. "This boy needs a lesson in manners."

The fist hit Napoleon, not once but many times. He fell to the ground and later remembered being kicked, again and again. As he lost consciousness, one of the voices said, "Come on, Tom . . . come on, he's not getting up."

When Napoleon came to, his head was throbbing and his face and hair were matted with blood. He was dizzy. His ribs ached, and getting up was agony. Finally he managed to throw himself across his horse and ride off toward the Riel house.

"*Enfant de chienne!*" Dumont cursed when he had heard Napoleon's story.

"Scott is one man who should stay out of Dumont's gun sight," said old Ouellette, shaking his head.

That was Monday, the first day of a long long week.

Julie Riel gave Napoleon her own bed and she was insistent that he was not to be moved from there. It was a high oak bed with four tall, sturdy posters. The mattress was stuffed with feathers, and the quilts that covered him were filled with goose down. Julie Riel was as proud of her bed as she was of anything she owned. Her husband had bought it in St. Paul and hauled it in a Red River cart all the way to St. Boniface. No one in the Red River had a bed as fine as hers, not even the fine English ladies in Fort Garry. The sheets, the quilts, even the down fillings had been the product of her own hands. This was a bed as fine as any in Ontario or Quebec, and she cherished it.

Lying in the huge bed, young Napoleon looked even smaller than he was, a pale, bruised face in a sea of heavily embroidered linen. His body sank into the quilts and appeared in danger of disappearing. Julie had wrapped his mid-section in stiff linen cloths. She knew his ribs were broken, and she had seen her mother do this when a man was thrown from a horse. The cuts on his face and legs were more serious. Napoleon had been out too long. One cut, which was quite deep—she thought Scott must have been wearing a heavy ring—had gone septic. Pus oozed from it and it pained the boy terribly.

Julie sent for one of the old Cree women to bring the drawing stones and the bark medicines. She described them in detail to Elzéar Goulet, who was sent to fetch the old lady. Together they worked on poor Napoleón, applying the hot poultices and reapplying new ones when the others had cooled. The old Indian woman, whose face was so lined it looked as though it had been carved from stone, softly sang incantations. Occasionally she emitted strange gurgling sounds from her throat. Julie Riel sang too. The Cree medicines drew poisons from the body, but the spirits which made them effective had to be summoned, for religion and medicine were one to the Cree. Hail Marys and prayers intermingled with Cree chants.

Tuesday, following the day Napoleon was so badly beaten, the Métis men held another meeting. It began in the afternoon and lasted until early evening.

Louis Riel was weary. His face was paler now and that made his eyes appear even larger. He had been working at his books. He was drafting the documents that would legally establish a provisional government for the territory. He knew that time was important, tempers were flaring and the famous Métis patience was running out. Violence, in spite of Napoleon's beating, must be avoided at all costs. Too much, far too much was at stake. All his intellect and reasoning told him that the Métis were right—now was the time. The Métis nation could become a reality. The Hudson's Bay Company, once an empire in its own right, had relinquished its ownership of the land, and the Canadian government had not yet seized its claim. No governor had been appointed, no troops could arrive in time, and Parliament had not acted. Indeed, if all his information was correct, it would not act until December, thought Riel. Until then, Red River was a no man's land populated by some six thousand Métis, the remaining Cree and other Indian tribes, and a few thousand English-speaking settlers. The

English-speakers were divided into the English, Irish, Canadians, and Americans.

James Wickes Taylor arrived in Fort Garry on Tuesday at mid-day. The bush telegraph, that unique mode of communication, had spread word of his arrival rapidly through the Métis. Taylor was on his way to meet Riel. The governor-designate, William McDougall, was laying over in St. Paul for a few days and Taylor had good reason to seek out this man, Riel, of whom he had heard so much.

When news of Napoleon Nault's beating reached him, he had abandoned his wagon and ridden hard. Moments like this were few and far between, he thought.

Taylor was coming from Pembina, the frontier settlement on the American side of the border. He had not enjoyed his stay in Pembina. It was a trying place for a city-bred lawyer from St. Paul via Washington. Taylor did not dislike the West, in any case it was not his job either to like or to dislike it. He was a man with a mission, a mission that just might work out, and he sensed the moment could be at hand.

"We could not at this time foresee committing troops, Mr. Taylor," Secretary of State Seward said in his deep, raspy voice.

Taylor thought Seward had remarkable powers of diplomacy and insight. People laughed about Alaska, but one day, he suspected, they would recognize its worth.

"How far should I take this then?" He looked at Seward and hoped the right answers would come from him. Taylor had a vision too—the Pacific Northwest from Alaska to the border under one flag, the stars and stripes. He wanted desperately to urge the Secretary to action. Every instinct he had clamored that it was now or never. It had to be now, now before the Canadians finished that stupid railway. If they finished it, he reasoned, and Alaska were to be developed, the Americans would have to get there via Canadian territory.

Right now the United States held all the cards. The Canadians couldn't get to their western frontier without going through the U.S.

"I want you to be my eyes and ears in the West, Mr. Taylor. I want you to forward information, plans, ideas, and assessments directly to me here at the State Department. I want you to urge the free people of the Red River to join us; more specifically, I want you to point up the wisdom of that decision." Seward leaned back and sipped some water.

"They might well make that decision, Mr. Secretary. But what if the British . . . or Canadians send troops?"

The Secretary smiled sarcastically. "They'll have a long walk, a very long walk, Mr. Taylor. Not one of them is going to come through the United States. No British Imperialist army is going to take one step in this country."

"And if they're Canadians?" asked Taylor.

"Same damn thing! God, it's bad enough having the French messing around in Mexico . . . and then there's Santo Domingo. No, Mr. Taylor, we can't commit troops, but I can promise you and your friends that the Canadians, or British, or whatever those people up there are, will have one hell of a time getting to the Red River."

Taylor was a happy man. Now he was ready, and the time was right. He would meet with the Métis and talk to this fellow Riel. The Secretary would be pleased, very pleased, with an election coming up.

Louis talked, cajoled, and pleaded. His arguments were solid. The other Métis had wanted to lay Scott out right then and there, but Louis said no. There were times one had to fight violence with violence, he said, and when that time came he would be the first to take up arms.

"We must commit an act of peaceful resistance," he told them.

"How about we let Scott's horse drag him to Pembina by a rope?" asked Goulet, grinning broadly at the thought.

In the end Dumont spoke up and surprised Louis by agreeing with him, suggesting they follow Louis' plan to stop the survey team, simply throwing a little scare into the English Canadians.

"Twelve riders, no more," Dumont suggested: Goulet, Lépine, old Ouellette, Tremblay, Nolin, Nault's two cousins, Bouchet, and two of the Lefevres, together with Dumont and Riel—who was insistent about coming— made up the twelve. All were armed, except Louis.

It did not take the group long to find the survey team. They were working about a mile from where they had attacked young Napoleon. The day was unusually warm for October. The sun had come up over the low rolling hills in a bright orange blaze. The tall grass, some of it still green, some of it turning brown, blew gently in the breeze. The first frost had already touched the leaves of the low trees and the scrub brushes. As the twelve riders reached the crest of the hill they looked down on a sea of colour populated only by the figures of the four surveyors and their wagon in the distance.

For a moment the group paused, and then Dumont lifted his arm skyward and gave the loud whooping yell of the Métis hunter as he charged the buffalo. The distant figures grew larger as they galloped. The four men froze in position like the people turned to salt in the legendary city of Sodom.

The horsemen drew to a sudden halt, reigning in their horses, and six of the riders dismounted.

The group of surveyors looked terrified, with the exception of Tom Scott. The face of fear, he had learned, should never be shown to a savage.

"Well, well . . ." Scott said slowly. He could easily dismiss the lot of ruffians as half-breed savages. One, however, puzzled him. He was obviously different from the others, the man dressed in the black garb of a cleric with his white, high, stiff collar.

"You don't belong here!" Goulet shouted.

"That's right! If we want a road here, we'll build it! *Mange de la merde, anglais!*" Lépine's words were venomous.

Scott ignored the insult and simply grinned. His words hissed through his yellow teeth, his face revealing his insolence. "Not anymore. Now this road goes where the government wants it."

Goulet spit in Scott's face. "That to your government!" Scott's fist automatically doubled. One of the other surveyors, Charles Mair, tugged at Scott's sleeve. "Let's get out of here, Tom . . ." Mair was pleading now.

Dumont cocked his gun. At least one of the fools had some sense, he thought.

Scott shook his arm loose from Mair and, turning to him hissed, "Shut up, you chicken!"

Then he turned to Charles Nolin. Nolin was a Métis, but he had some education and a lot of friends among the Canadians. He was "their" Métis, a young, semiliterate who had ambitions of his own. "Charles Nolin, you're a Métis with a lot of friends in the Canada Firsters. You ought to know better than this."

Nolin blushed.

Blood is thicker than water, Dumont thought to himself. At least he thought it was. He himself did not like Nolin much and he wasn't sure exactly what ran through the man's veins. It might just turn out to be water.

Scott's instinct told him that Charles Nolin was the weak link. "This road is government business. You know better than to interfere with that."

Riel stepped forward and purposely broke Scott's line of vision to Nolin. He spoke firmly and calmly, in reasonably good English. He had an accent, but it was the kind of accent a cultured Frenchman might have.

It betrayed both his education and his years of study. Indeed, his use of English was superior to Scott's. Scott, Louis knew, had been born to his English, but he was uneducated.

"It's not what you're doing that matters!" Louis began, "It's that you've got no right to do *anything* here! Your government hasn't taken over yet!"

This made Scott very uneasy. Louis looked at him as though he were beneath contempt.

"And what's that supposed to mean?" he asked. He knew damn well the government hadn't taken over yet, but of course it was only a matter of time.

Louis' eyes held the man and then dropped him as one might drop a squirming snake. "It means that you're a *liar*." Dumont smiled.

Scott stepped back. Idiots. Probably just worried about continued supplies of whisky. Maybe he could sooth them with a promise. "Look," he began. "this land is all going to Canada and every one of you'll be looked after."

"Like Napoleon Nault, the boy you beat yesterday?" Louis asked.

Scott sneered and turned to face one of his survey crew. "MacAndrews, move that chain fifty yards west!" Giving the order made him feel better, but MacAndrews was petrified. "I said, move it!" Scott yelled. His own voice surprised him, its pitch higher than usual.

Nolin stepped up to Louis and said, "Louis, maybe we shouldn't . . . Well, we don't know what's going to happen." Water, Dumont thought, that man needs watching.

Louis instantly moved sideways and stood on the chain that MacAndrews had been ordered to move. Goulet moved in behind him, planting his feet on the chain too. Then, Lépine, Tremblay, and the others who had dismounted did the same.

"Get the hell off that chain, you dirty half-breeds!" Scott's voice boomed. One of the surveyors drew his gun, but Dumont levelled his own rifle at the man. "I shoot off your trigger finger, one of your two eyes out—or maybe something lower, eh?" The surveyor dropped his gun. Gabriel Dumont never missed. Somebody else could build this road, the man thought. After all, he had a young wife to satisfy.

Mair and MacAndrews were now pulling Scott toward the wagon. Scott's courage was by now failing him too, and he let himself be pulled away.

"*Va chez ta putain!*" old Ouellette called out, remembering the scene he and Dumont had witnessed between Scott and Mrs. Schultz.

The surveyors' wagon moved across the field slowly, bumping as the wheels passed over the uneven ground. "Stupid half-breed savages," Scott was mumbling over and over. "Just don't have enough sense to listen to reason. Why couldn't they get it through their thick heads that land was meant to be developed, used, made profitable?

Maudits anglais! Dumont thought, as the riders headed for their rendezvous with the other Métis representatives. Why couldn't these Canadian English realize that this was Métis land, that the Métis would look after them? Yes, even with justice.

7

What's Not Nailed Down . . .

In the history of thought and culture, the dark nights have perhaps in some ways cost mankind less grief than the false dawns.

Louis Kronenberger

James Wickes Taylor was known in Fort Garry. He had taken the time and the trouble to establish a number of friendships among the Canadian English. After all, a man in his profession had to know everything. How these people felt and acted, as well as what they planned was important. From them, as well as from Canadian officials passing through Pembina and St. Paul, he had kept track of what was happening in Ottawa.

William McDougall, who it seems had been promised the governorship by that Tory politician Macdonald, had been in St. Paul for over a week. He had drunk a lot and he talked even more. The man, of course, had no power yet—he was a gesture, a symbol of things to come.

Maybe, just maybe, Taylor reasoned, that Canadian Prime Minister was not entirely idiotic. A smart man always put his toe in the water before he plunged in. Maybe McDougall was the Prime Minister's toe. He laughed to himself—more the Prime Minister's ass actually.

"Tact," Mr. Seward had said. Well, tactful he would be. Everyone in Fort Garry knew he came to Canada frequently on business. However, not everyone knew of his friendship with the Métis. It would be better, much better, if he saw this Riel alone before the meeting. It might get around if he, an American "businessman," were off conspiring with the Métis. Certainly not all of them could be trusted either. Charles Nolin, that pussyfooting little mission-educated one, had his own plans to become the Métis spokesman in the Parliament . . . if indeed anyone in the territory ever voted for Parliamentary representation, or was allowed to. Nolin, however, might have been only one of three or four who couldn't be trusted. Nothing in his intelligence information suggested that the French Métis as a whole were anything like divided in their sentiments.

The English Métis, on the other hand, were another matter. They were split right down the centre. That was because they were only half a minority. Half-breeds to be sure, but they spoke English, not French. The Irishmen from Ontario and Ireland would certainly support the Métis and this fellow Riel. It was the Fenians on both sides of the border who were the real troublemakers. They hated the Orangemen who ran Ontario. Besides, the Irish settlers were Catholic and the Catholics stuck together like glue. A trifle dangerous, because they kept getting their government tangled up with their church, but of course that sort of thing could be controlled. Even some of the English settlers wouldn't support annexation. No doubt about it, this fellow Riel had all the cards. James Wickes Taylor thought he'd give Mr. Riel another wild one. A Royal Flush was certainly better than four of a kind.

Taylor checked into the Fort Garry hotel. Hardly anything like the Ritz in Washington, he thought, but one had to have a base of operations. Staying in the spare room offered him on previous visits by the "good" doctor's wife, Mrs. Schultz, might prove a little tricky this time. In any case, this trip was for business, not idle distraction. The hotel was a wooden structure two stories high. It boasted twelve fine, fully furnished rooms.

The lobby could have been the lobby of any frontier establishment, although Fort Garry was nowhere near as rough and ready a place as Pembina. For one thing, there were no prostitutes in the hotel. One had to leave and go elsewhere for that sort of thing. It did have a bar, but compared to other western towns it was a quiet place. The English, Taylor knew, had their own parties. They were closet lushes. The Métis drank in the saddle so to speak. They probably had their own places too, under the stars.

The room had a narrow, clean bed with embroidered, down-filled quilts, a single wooden rocker, and a plain and obviously handmade dresser. The floor was bare wood, except for a single Indian mat beside the bed.

By noon, Taylor, again on horseback, was approaching the Riel homestead.

The woman who opened the door looked to be about fifty. Taylor thought how beautiful she must have been twenty years before. She dressed like a Métis, but she was slender, fine boned, and almost delicate looking. She directed him to her son, who was poring over some papers.

"My name is James Taylor," he said, extending his hand. The pale, intense young man shook it.

"Some friends have spoken to me about you," said Riel. "You're a 'trader,' from Pembina."

Something in the way Riel said "trader" made him think his friends were quite perceptive.

"I am . . ." Taylor paused, choosing his words carefully, "an interested party, a friend to the Métis people both here and in the United States." That part was certainly true. He had many Métis friends on the other side of the border.

Riel appraised the man before him and found he liked his ready smile and direct manner. He had known few Americans, but he had liked them all. He could sense the man meant well. He thought he would make it easier for him to get to the point. His own intelligence reports had given him to understand that Taylor had good connections in Washington. He did not particularly want to end up American himself, but a little of the right kind of pressure could only help his planned demonstration of strength. Riel wanted a Métis nation, perhaps a Métis province, but definitely not a Métis state. Everything he knew about the actions of powerful nations told him that independence was best achieved—and maintained—when two powerful nations were in a stalemate, counter-balancing one another.

"Please sit down, Mr. Taylor. Let me tell you about our plans . . ."

This may be easier than I thought, Taylor thought to himself.

Riel told him about establishing a government for the territory—pre-empting the Parliament and forcing the Canadians to negotiate. "We," he concluded, "will be the provisional government. We will be in a legal position, even under English law. They will have to listen to us."

"They could send in troops," Taylor suggested.

"Could they?" Riel asked. There was a twinkle in his eye. Uncharacteristic for one so intense, so serious.

"I can't say too much, Mr. Riel. Yes, they could send in troops, but I am told they would have a long walk."

Riel's smile changed his whole face. It was the broad, understanding grin of a man who has grasped the essence of a situation very quickly.

Americans play international poker, Riel thought. It will be their downfall in a world of chess players.

Taylor rose and he and Riel shook hands. "Good luck with the Canadians," he said. As he left the Riel house, Taylor felt some satisfaction. He couldn't be sure what way Riel would move, but certain possibilities seemed quite strong. He might well choose to negotiate with the Canadian government first, but knowing what he did of the Canadian Prime Minister, Macdonald, Taylor could not imagine the negotiations being fruitful.

The English and the French had such language problems! The Americans, on the other hand, knew that people who wanted to do business quickly learned sufficient English to manage. Past that, they never gave language a second thought.

When Taylor had departed, Louis prepared himself for the meeting. He gathered his notes and set out. Even he could not imagine how long the journey he was just beginning would last. Today's meeting was the first step toward a preordained fate.

As Louis approached the church, he prepared himself mentally. It would go as he had planned, he told himself. The representatives would listen, they would consider the arguments. People would speak for and against, they would waiver, but in the end they would stand where they believed their best interests to be. In Métis culture, the group was everything, it spoke with a collective mind, it acted as a body.

Father Ritchot's prairie church looked warm and friendly. Many horses were tied outside, and five or six wagons stood in various places near the front. It could have been a special celebration, or even a Sunday-morning mass. He glanced at the cemetery where his father was buried, the place he had so recently visited on his way home. He wondered if the ghost of the Dreamer still hovered over the spot.

"I have returned, father." He said it out loud. The Dreamer had been right, dead warriors do return.

He walked into the church where they were all waiting, then down the centre aisle, head bowed. Eyes followed him. Louis dropped to his knees at the altar rail and crossed himself. Behind him he heard the others. Following his example, they too bowed their heads in prayer. He knelt a long time; he had much to talk to God about this day. The sunlight streamed through the window. It fell on the altar and illuminated it in a heavenly light. Louis stared and stared at the figure of

Christ on the cross. He was transfixed, a statue in prayer, God's tool, his messenger, his servant.

Louis blinked; the sunlight seemed very strong indeed. A pain, sudden and piercing, jabbed through his head. His temples throbbed. He hadn't had such an attack in many months now, but he knew it would pass quickly. As he stared at Christ on the cross, a cloud began to move across the sun and the light lessened momentarily. Eyes wide, the lips of the Christ seemed to move. Louis let out a breath. Was God intending to speak to him? He waited. Nothing.

Dumont, who had been dragged into church by the others, reluctantly crossed himself and said a short prayer. Many of the men continued to pray silently with Louis, others looked on respectfully.

"Louis certainly spends a long time at his prayers," Dumont whispered to Tremblay, who was looking on but not praying.

"It might help," he answered.

"Well, it can't hurt," Dumont said, shrugging.

At last Louis stood and faced the group, and the meeting began. The riders had returned with representatives from every Métis area. They also brought with them William B. O'Donoghue, a known Fenian sympathizer who would represent the Irish settlers, and Robert Mathews, an English settler who represented those with misgivings about the Canadians and their political party, the Canada Firsters. The English Métis too sent representatives, four in all. Thus, all factions were represented, as Louis had hoped. There was no disputing the fact that together they represented the majority of the people in the territory.

He went through his plan slowly and patiently. He thoroughly explained their right to form a governing council, to represent themselves, to establish a provisional government. He concentrated on the law of nations and on possible Canadian reaction. He was brilliant, Dumont thought. His voice was strong and resonant, his words clear and impassioned. He chose each one well, and for the benefit of the Irish and English representatives, he translated. The Métis representatives who had not yet encountered this man were impressed. They hung on his words as if in a trance. Here was a leader, here was a man who could speak for them.

When he had finished, they shouted their questions as he had known they would. He clarified points, and re-explained others for those who required simpler explanations.

Michel Dumas rose and shouted, "What if the Canadians send troops?"

Louis smiled. He had been waiting for the question. "I am told . . ." He paused. "I have information—that the Americans will not allow Canadian troops to cross U.S. territory."

There was a whoop and a holler that resounded throughout the little church. Dumont was on his feet.

"We can keep them out forever. If they walk from Ontario, they'll be in no condition to fight!"

More cheers and wild yelling. The Métis understood. They had a real advantage.

Shorty thereafter they approved a document setting out the terms of the provisional government's entry into Confederation, ard they elected a council of twelve to act for the new government, among them, William O'Donoghue. Among the terms included was the right to elect a legislature that could override a veto by the Executive; the right to approve or reject, through the territory's representative, any Dominion legislation that directly affected the territory; the right to elect sheriffs, magistrates, and other local officials; a free homestead law, land grants for schools, roads, and public buildings; a guaranteed railroad connection to the nearest existing line in the United States; use of the French and English languages in the legislature and in all public documents and in the courts; respect for all privileges, usages, and

72

customs that existed before the transfer of sovereignty; full and fair representation in the Parliament of the Dominion of Canada, and the promise of provincial status.

In their final decision the group agreed that Father Ritchot should take the document to Ottawa. Louis explained that one of his American friends was arranging the trip. Ritchot would leave for St. Paul the next day and from there he would take the American railway to Toronto. He might be in Ottawa by the end of the week if all went well.

Ottawa first, Father Ritchot thought, then on to Montreal to see the Bishop.

8

Ottawa Rebuffed

The turtle lays thousands of eggs without anyone knowing, but when the hen lays one egg, the country is informed.

A Malay proverb

Governor-designate William McDougall felt he had tarried in St. Paul a bit too long. The Americans had arranged so much for him, so many parties. How could he refuse? He felt reassured now that Scott and the surveyor, Mair, had come to meet him and take him to Fort Garry. He simply hated being escorted by Métis guides from Pembina. There was simply nothing he could talk to them about!

What a godforsaken country this was, McDougall thought. The whole place was full of Indians and half-breeds, prostitutes and liquor. God, he hoped Fort Garry would not be the same. After the night spent in Pembina, he yearned for a comfortable bed, a little brandy, and some pleasant conversation. God knows, the poor people in Red River needed him and the authority vested in him. But he was troubled. Scott and Mair had mentioned a little "difficulty" with the Métis. Well, *he* was not going to have any difficulty with those people. After all, Sir John A. Macdonald, the Prime Minister of Canada, had sent him as his personal envoy. This was to be, finally, his chance to govern, and of course his first duty would be to reassure the Métis and their meddling priests that they would get their due. Whatever their due was, he could not imagine.

They rode in an arrow-like formation, with Riel and Dumont at their head. The tall grass was flattened by the hoofs of the horses as the early morning sun shone over their shoulders. These were the Métis people as they had always been, as they were, as they always hoped to be. Horsemen of the plains, like the gauchos of the Pampas and the cowboys of the American southwest. They were the new cossacks of a new land, a new race, a race born of two peoples who were now one. All, save Riel, rode easy in the saddle, completely at home.

Coming over the hill they saw McDougall's buggy, its black top absorbing the sun and its four thin wheels bouncing along unevenly on the narrow pitted road. Charles Mair and Tom Scott rode alongside. McDougall's ample baggage could be seen piled behind the single seat.

The horsemen galloped up and the buggy expectantly stopped as they approached. McDougall rose to greet the riders. A scruffy looking bunch, he thought.

Dumont spoke first. "Mr. McDougall?"

McDougall was relieved at hearing so polite a salutation. He did not hear the sarcasm in Dumont's voice.

"Indeed, my good man, indeed?" McDougall patted his oversized stomach and caressed his gold watch chain.

"We read you a little paper, eh?" Dumont tilted his head toward Louis, who was unrolling a piece of paper.

How nice, McDougall thought, they've come out to greet their new governor. Really! Those surveyors must be quite mad.

Meanwhile Scott and Mair moved cautiously to either side of the buggy. Dumont met Scott's look and smiled. Mair was once again terrified.

Riel began reading in a loud and clear voice while McDougall tilted his head and grinned stupidly.

"Sir: We the newly formed National Committee of the Métis of Red River, order William McDougall . . ."

Up to this point McDougall had been smiling. He was wearing a monocle in his left eye. The smile abruptly left his face when he heard the word "order," and the monocle dropped to his stomach.

". . . not to enter the territory of the Northwest without special permission of the above-mentioned committee . . . By order of the General Secretary, Louis Riel."

McDougall had not noticed the horsemen fan out and form a barrier, with Riel and Dumont remaining at the centre. Laboriously he climbed down out of the carriage and walked over to Scott.

"What the hell are you getting me into?" he whispered to Scott. "Good God, I could have stayed in St. Paul a few more days and let the Canadian Firsters clean up this mess. How the hell could they run a territory if they couldn't handle a few half-breeds?"

Scott did not look at McDougall, because it would have meant looking down and away from the gaze of Dumont.

"They have no right to stop you, sir." He said it loudly, and he said it to Dumont.

McDougall was tugging at Scott's sleeve. By now Scott was angry and a little frustrated. He bent to acknowledge the pudgy little hand that begged for his attention.

"Perhaps we'd best wait till my commission is actually . . ." McDougall paused to lower his voice to a total whisper. "Legal."

Scott straightened himself up. "They're bluffing, Governor! Early or not, they wouldn't dare take on the Governor!" For a moment he half believed it himself, but then he remembered the incident with the surveyors' chain. Christ, he hardly knew who he hated most, that savage Dumont, Riel, who could have passed for white but chose to cast his lot with the half-breeds, or the snivelling excuse for a man he had just called "Governor."

McDougall shook like a wet dog just emerged from a puddle. He waddled up to Riel, turning his ankle on a loose stone as he did so.

"You, move out of the blasted way!" McDougall hollered, in his most imperious tone.

The riders began moving fiercely toward Mair and Scott. Two shots were fired in the air and a heavy rope stung the back of Mair and Scott's horses. The Métis riders let out a resounding whoop and Scott and Mair took off for their lives to the north. The Métis set off in mock pursuit with every intention of driving the two men in an easterly direction and getting them lost along one of the hidden smuggling trails.

McDougall now extended a scroll to Riel and Dumont and the remaining Métis. "This is a commission from the Prime Minister of Canada!" He was shrieking hysterically. "Stop this now!"

Dumont saw the boxes of champagne in the back of the buggy and a smile broke over his face. Maybe, he thought, this political stuff of Riel's had some good things to offer. The buffalo were disappearing; maybe he could take up hunting governors! Ripping open the box with one hand, he began tossing the bottles of champagne to his riders. Some of them caught their bounty on the gallop, while all laughed heartily.

McDougall's face was red and puffy and he looked as though he might actually cry.

"You can't do this! That's my private property!"

Dumont spied a bottle that one of the riders had missed. It was lying on the ground in one piece, having landed nicely on a bed of flattened grass. He rode over, first circling in a wide arc, and then, leaning from his saddle gallantly scooped up the bottle. He rode over to the governor and ceremoniously handed it to him.

"My compliments, Monsieur, I understand it's quite good, even though it tickles the nose, eh?"

With that Lépine turned the horses about and two horsemen lifted the astounded governor more or less upside down into the back of the buggy. They slapped the horses and the buggy jerked sharply off toward the American border.

"*Au revoir*," Gabriel shouted. He had bitten the cork out of one of the bottles and now raised it in a final toast to the departing governor, whose feet could be seen flailing wildly in the air. Then he turned to Riel, who was smiling, and lifted the bottle toward him. "To the Métis nation! To Louis Riel! To the finest horsemen ever to hunt the *anglais* buffalo!" Then the whole party turned, laughing, and rode off toward Fort Garry.

The flag they designed for their new nation was a blue *fleur de lis* flanked by a harp and shamrock, on a white background. Louis himself was not sure about the flag. He knew that symbols were important, but he also realized the importance of negotiation. William O'Donoghue also troubled Riel. That man, he reasoned, could cause many problems in the weeks ahead.

The late hours of the afternoon were spent meeting with the committee. Because Scott and Mair had been allowed to ride off, news would soon reach the Canada Firsters in Fort Garry. It was unimportant, however, because tonight the Métis would proclaim Fort Garry the new capital of their new nation, "Manitoba."

Elzéar Goulet climbed the wall shortly after dark and swung open the gates of the fort. The Métis horsemen rode unopposed through the gates, some one hundred strong. More quickly followed, and before anyone in the fort knew it, the post was theirs. Soon bonfires lighted the entire square of the fort. Tall timbers reached upward, forming the skeleton of a teepee, and flames danced along them, leaping high into the night. The Métis were in full regalia for their victory celebrations— embroidered moccasins, buckskins, and colourful shirts and headbands of deep red, gold, blue, and green. Dark eyes danced merrily in the night and the sounds of the fiddle and flute carried into the still night air. There was wild dancing, the step-dancing brought so long ago, first from France to Quebec, and then across the wild prairies. The songs, the poetry of the wilderness, echoed through Fort Garry, the voices crashing against the walls. The dances had made their long journey to Red River with the French *coureurs de bois*, from the settlements of Quebec, where they had given heart to the people. Then they crept along the shores of the St. Lawrence, through the woods of Upper Canada, then the valleys along the shores of Lake Superior, and finally burst forth onto the great plains. Here, little changed, the songs were nurtured and preserved by the Métis. They were the songs that told of oppression, of war, of liberation— and now of the Métis nation. The Métis, a new breed, had tossed off their bonds and tonight they celebrated!

They ran the new flag up the pole and toasted it with drink and song. Then, as Riel had anticipated he might, O'Donoghue, when the others were momentarily distracted, brought it down and ran up the stars and stripes. Riel himself stepped forward to bring it down. The time was not right, he reasoned, negotiations were necessary if the Métis advantage were to hold. Finally, he ran up the Union Jack and the new Métis flag, while the American flag was set aside. The Americans had their use, but they were too strong to negotiate with. Besides, the Sioux had learned what their treaties meant.

The settlers huddled in Dr. Schultz's house could not see which flag was flying, but at that point none of them much cared. Mrs. Schultz was the bravest of the lot. She came out onto the veranda of her fine Victorian house and surveyed the scene in the square.

"You half-breed barbarians! You'll never get away with this!" she shouted, but her words were lost in the dancing and the music. She hurled a stone at the revelers.

Dumont had both seen and heard her. "*La putain!*" he shouted, and spying a flowerpot near her on the corner, took aim and fired. It shattered into bits and crashed to the ground. With that, Mrs. Schultz ran screaming back into the house.

"*Maudit femme anglaise*," muttered Dumont. He wondered if she was that noisy in bed.

"Are you all right, Elizabeth?" one of the women asked as she entered.

"I'm just fine!" she spat, brushing her dress off.

With all the terrifying screaming and yelling going on outside, the two women who were in the Schultz house would not go home. Their husbands were away and they would not stay alone, so Tom Scott offered to remain for the night. He had not had the slightest intention of leaving anyway. After all, he reasoned, the doctor would not be home for a few days, and one ought to make the most of one's time. Mrs. Schultz had the two women sleep in the guest room next to the living room. One of the upstairs bedrooms was assigned to Scott, but Mrs. Schultz knew it would remain empty.

Once the two women were shown to their room and settled in, Mrs. Schultz met Scott in the hallway, and with a seductive glance took his hand and led him upstairs to the master bedroom. Scott took off his coat and shoes, then the rest of his clothes, and reclined on the bed with his hands behind his head watching her undress. She did it slowly, and that aroused him.

Later, having spent himself, Scott slowly sank into a deep sleep. His last thoughts were of that stupid bumbling governor and of his being chased for miles by those mad savages.

He did not remember dreaming, but he knew he had been deeply asleep.

"Kill him! Kill him! Kill him!" Mrs. Schultz was screaming and shaking him.

He came to and shook his head in bewilderment.

"Kill him!" she repeated, staring wildly at him. She just kept saying it over and over. Then she got out of bed, and naked, walked across the floor to get his rifle. "Kill Riel!"

He took the rifle from her. "Yes," he said, not because she demanded it, but because he knew it must be done.

"But it can't be done right away!" He looked at her with fear and caution in his eyes. "The time isn't right— I have to get some help."

"What about me? What about me?" Her voice was near hysteria, shrill, demanding.

"You'll have to stay here, Elizabeth."

"With those savages out there dancing in the streets and setting fires? They'll kill us all!" she screeched.

"Hardly." Scott felt stronger now, and having slept a little, realized that *he* was the one in danger. He couldn't think why he had come back at all. He should have kept on going. "Look," he said, taking one of her hands in his, "they're just celebrating their little victory. In the morning they'll be gone. Life will go on as usual."

She withdrew her hand from his and wrapped the sheet around herself. "And then what?"

"You'll send those women back to their own house, you'll behave as you always do, and you'll wait."

She knew he was right. She knew the Métis wouldn't hurt her and that in time she would have her way. This was just a setback, and of course it was a little frightening. "Yes," she answered. "But you *will* kill him?"

"I'll put a bullet right through his heart." She smiled at his answer. "But it will take some time, some planning. It could take a couple of weeks—they're looking for me now. You remember the Nault boy—well, some of them are pretty mad. I'll have to go south for a week or two, try to find Evans and get some help."

"My husband's in Ottawa now. Surely they'll do something there. They did make us promises when we came out here, Tom."

"Of course the government will do something! Good God, look what those savages did to McDougall this morning!"

"When will you kill him? He's the cause of everything."

"One night. I'll get him, but right now it's too soon. They'd be expecting it now. Let them think they've won, let them be the authority in the territory for a couple of weeks. Let *them* feel confident. Then one night I'll get that bloody savage."

Scott went to the window and looked out. The square was empty now and the bonfire was a bed of glowing coals. The fiddles had ceased playing and the dancers had gone home. Bits of broken glass littered the streets and papers could be seen blowing against the sides of the buildings. The Union Jack and the Métis flag fluttered limply on the flagpole.

9

Macdonald's Man in the West

A non-violent revolution is not a program of seizure of power. It is a program of transformation of relationships.

Gandhi

The fine shiny carriage carrying Dr. Schultz and Donald Smith moved slowly up Ottawa's Wellington Street. The horses hoofs clanged as they crossed the bridge over the Rideau Canal, its waters placid and reflecting the grey, sunless skies above. "The Hill" rose up on the left and behind it the Ottawa River lazed into the distance. The Houses of Parliament stood majestically on the endless expanse of browning grass, a lonely citadel from which the heart of a new nation was beginning to beat. The great glass windows looked to the south and the west and down on the tiny French village of Hull located on the river's lower side.

Most of the trees were already bare, but a few bright orange and yellow leaves still clung to the maple trees. They held onto life with a kind of desperation and shook in the cold north winds. The uniformed driver pulled his coat around him. It was nearly the first of November, and the gathering clouds gave warning that this year at least, there would be no Indian summer.

"My wife, a delicate, gentle lady, and my friends are now virtually held captive by these hooligans!"

Dr. Schultz was holding the latest in a series of letters from his wife. Smith wondered how captives could send so many letters and why the protective doctor, who was now residing in some luxury at the Queen Victoria Hotel, was not at his wife's side. He stroked his long beard and feigned a tone of deep concern.

"An unfortunate situation, Dr. Schultz." Politics was definitely not his game. It was true that he felt the situation unfortunate, not unexpected, just unfortunate. On the other hand he did not regard Mrs. Schultz's situation as unfortunate.

Schultz pulled himself upright. His voice was now more demanding. "Unfortunate? It is a dangerous and demeaning situation! Now what action does our government intend to take to protect them?"

Smith sucked in his breath slowly and closed his eyes tightly—the man simply had no understanding, he thought. His prejudice clouded his vision; it was like talking to a brick wall. He was supremely sorry that Schultz and Scott and the others were the leaders of a political party whose support Ottawa needed. The other English-speaking settlers seemed calm enough. They had their limitations too, but most of them knew the Métis better.

"The Métis don't harm their captives, Dr. Schultz. It's not part of their culture." He wondered why he bothered. Schultz did not recognize that the Métis even had a culture.

"What about Louis Riel?" the doctor demanded. "He's civilized!"

Smith smiled. "Oh, that could make him dangerous."

The doctor was not amused. Smith brought his hands together, folded them, and placed each of his forefingers on either side of his nose. It was his thinking position. Yes, yes he thought, civilized men could be dangerous indeed.

"When we were encouraged to settle in the territory, we assumed certain guarantees . . . promises were made to us . . ." Dr. Schultz's voice trailed off as the carriage came to a halt in front of the East block.

"I'll be discussing this with the Prime Minister this evening," Smith said to Schultz.

"Every day counts." Schultz looked at him anxiously.

"Yes" said Smith, knowing full well that each of those days helped cool off the situation. He remembered the Prime Minister's favourite saying: "We do not give a standing ovation after the first act of a play. We wait until all the actors have given their full performances." Time was certainly an important factor. The full scenario should be known, everybody's actions, present and future, should be assessed. The Prime Minister weighed and he balanced, he thought and he acted, he had a vision, and no one was going to obstruct its becoming a reality.

The billiards room was oak panelled, with high walls on which hung paintings depicting hunting scenes. On the far wall a portrait of Her Majesty hung alone, demanding attention and commanding respect. The deep green felt of the mahogany billiard table was covered with the multicoloured balls. Sir John was holding a cue in his hands as Smith entered. The Prime Minister straightened up. His lean face smiled his half-smile.

"Take a cue, Donald." He motioned toward the cue rack in the corner.

"Sir John . . ." Donald held the latest complaint from McDougall in his hand.

"I read his dispatch. Poor McDougall, he's been festering in St. Paul now for nearly a month," said Sir John, mockingly. Poor McDougall!

"Tell me about this Riel. Tell me who he is, but more importantly, can he be dealt with?" The Prime Minister was edging toward a decision. He wanted his own suspicions confirmed.

"He's a Métis," Smith began, "but he was educated in Quebec. A protégé, I understand, of Bishop Bourget."

The Prime Minister looked interested. "Of Bishop Bourget? Oh, one of those."

"Not necessarily," Smith began. "One can't be sure

he subscribes to Ultramontanism. One can't even be entirely sure the Bishop does—"

"To restore the medieval Catholic spirit and the union of Church and State, the political power subordinate. Dangerous ideas those."

Smith was not surprised that Sir John was so well informed. The Prime Minister was a quiet, brooding man with an explosive temper and a shrewd mind. He made it his business to know everything that could possibly affect his plans for the country.

"Well, Donald," the Prime Minister continued, "you know the territory and the natives. How serious is it? Are troops required?"

Sir John reached for the glass of scotch and took a large swallow. He had no intention of sending troops, at least for the moment, and wondered how his friend would answer.

"If you send troops west, you'd best reserve a battalion to quiet Montreal as well."

The Prime Minister's eyes sparkled. "Armed resistance in Montreal in protest over the Bishop's protégé? He sounds like more than a *mere* protégé to me!"

"Just a possible result, Sir John. One of many I'm afraid." Smith lined up his shot and sank the red ball neatly in the corner pocket.

"Well done Donald! I believe you're a natural!"

Smith straightened up. "Do you mind?" He nodded toward the bottle of scotch on the table.

"Certainly not," the Prime Minister responded. "The glasses are over there with the ice." He motioned toward the mahogany sideboard. Donald poured himself a drink and returned to the issue. "He's controllable, Sir John. He's concerned primarily about the Métis land rights."

"Aren't we all! Troops would be a very bad political move."

"Quite uncalled for at this point," Smith agreed with relief.

"And what *is* called for, Donald?" The Prime Minister turned to face him directly.

Smith thought for a moment. He was quite confident that he himself could straighten out the whole mess. "As you said, I know the Métis."

Sir John nodded again. "How long would it take you?"

Smith wasn't really sure himself. It called for diplomacy, fairness, and action. Somehow he was certain that this Riel fellow wanted to have the territory remain under British rule. "Not long," he answered, but his answer lacked conviction, and he wondered if the Prime Minister had detected his lack of firmness.

"I need your help, Donald. 'Our' railroad needs your help."

This time Smith's voice was totally confident. "It will not reach the Pacific until the West is secure, Sir John."

The Prime Minister looked at Donald Smith. "Politics, Donald, often consists of choosing between the disastrous and the distasteful. Be quick, Donald. Calm the troubled waters and knock Dumont and Riel right out of Fort Garry! Out of the whole territory if necessary!"

The disastrous and the distasteful. Smith wondered where the word "possible" fitted in. Sir John had gone back to his game and his drink. The subject was obviously closed.

The Prime Minister leaned on his cue. Time, time. Time was so damned important. It was nearly the first of November. Soon the House would be in Christmas recess . . . Damn Louis Riel! Whoever and whatever he was. Damn! That cleric-trained Métis had made a very shrewd political move . . . too shrewd for a mere protégé of the Bishop.

10

What Can Go Wrong, Will

In a democracy, the general good is furthered only when the special interests of competing minorities accidently coincide—or cancel each other out.

Alexander Chase

Just hours after Donald Smith had arrived at Fort Garry, the Métis had arranged a meeting in the town square. Smith hoped to speak to the crowd, but circumstances overtook his reason; he was seen with Dr. and Mrs. Schultz and was immediately placed on the side of one of the factions. Riel began—

"The Council of the Northwest has formally declared a provisional government to investigate and protect the rights of the people of this settlement . . ." Riel paused and looked at the Canada Firsters' faction and then continued, ". . . all of the people. It is a government which is now the only authority in the territory."

"Bloody treason!" Schultz was shaking his fist. Smith wished he could have persuaded Schultz to remain in Ottawa, but the doctor had returned with him.

"On the contrary, Dr. Schultz. According to the law of nations, our position is legal," Riel responded.

The Métis representatives cheered—all except O'Donoghue, who did not move. Smith could tell that the Irish and the Métis had had a falling out. Well, he thought, at least there's one crack in the wall of solidarity.

"I hold myself ready to conclude arrangements with

the Canadian government, if I judge them favourable to us all. Métis, Indians, English, all of us."

Mrs. Anderson yelled at Riel. "You'll try to keep us Canadians out!"

Riel answered her calmly. "Why should we? The Métis know what it means to be looked on as second class. Why should we believe that anyone would like that any better than we do? There is enough land here for all, and no need to fight over it."

Smith found himself agreeing with Riel. Why indeed, he wondered? His eyes swept over the expanse of rolling prairie in the distance.

"Who the hell picked you to tell us what to do?" It was MacAndrews. World enough and time, Smith thought. Mostly time.

Riel looked steadily at MacAndrews, a slight smile on his face. "Join me at mass this Sunday, Mr. Mac-Andrews, and you can ask God that question." The Métis all laughed.

"Father Ritchot has taken our demands to Ottawa."

"Demands!" Mrs. Schultz was red from her trim ankles to the top of her head.

Riel looked at her. "Yes, demands. Title to our own lands! Full provincial status. Money for schools!"

Mrs. Schultz stepped forward. "What will they teach? French? Cree? Or gobbledegook? And what will you do if the government sends troops and tries to enter the territory?"

Riel looked at her, then down at the ground and said a short prayer to himself. He measured his words carefully. "That would constitute an invasion, Mrs. Schultz. I would take up arms to repel it."

"My God!" one of the Canadians gasped, "It's sedition . . . the savages will kill us all!"

Schultz looked sharply at Smith. "And you think you're going to reason with these half-breeds?"

The Prime Minister had sent Ottawa to the Métis, in the person of his friend, Donald Smith, but at that point hardly anyone knew he was there. Things got to be such a mess in the square that Smith couldn't even step forward. The Canadians threw rocks and bottles at the Métis and there was much screaming and yelling. Dumont quickly moved in to protect Riel. Shots were fired above everyone's head. The numbers were staggering. Mostly women and children against two or three hundred Métis armed and on horseback. That they weren't all killed was due largely to Dumont, although he suspected that the Métis felt no need to silence mouths with bullets. He should have gone directly to Dumont or Riel then, but he made a terrible mistake and instead went home with Dr. Schultz. Some of the Canadians ran for their own houses, but about twenty-five took shelter in the Schultz house as well. They were now all holed up together.

Smith decided to wait with the rest of them until things calmed down. Then he announced that he must go to Riel.

"You can't go." Mrs. Schultz was insistent. "They wouldn't dare attack us with the Prime Minister's personal envoy here."

"My dear lady," he replied, "at this moment nobody knows I am the Prime Minister's personal envoy."

"Oh yes," she said, rather sheepishly.

Smith took a white flag, just in case, but it didn't prove necessary. He opened the door slowly and walked out the front door. Goulet watched the lone, bearded figure as he approached. The horsemen behind him talked casually among themselves as Smith strode up to Goulet.

"I am Donald Smith." He extended his hand to the puzzled Métis. "I've come from Ottawa to talk to Louis Riel." Goulet smiled and pointed to the Hudson's Bay post down the street. Smith strode unmolested toward the trading post.

Louis Riel and Donald Smith talked well into the night. Riel, Smith discovered, was more than a religious fanatic on a mission. The young man had as sharp a political mind as he had ever encountered. Clearly, Riel was first and foremost a humanitarian. He cared about his people, but he was far from indifferent toward others. That he was stubborn on many points did not surprise him. And, when all was said and done, Riel was willing to talk terms. Some of his ideas were impractical, but where Riel was impractical, Dumont stepped in. Dumont, Smith thought, was one of the most likeable men he had ever met. Straightforward, and a leader himself. Riel could lead men's minds, but not their bodies. Dumont could organize and lead men, but he could not direct their minds. These two were a formidable pair, something to be reckoned with. In the end they agreed to meet again in the morning.

Smith walked back toward the Schultz house. He really hadn't counted on what happened next.

"Well?" Schultz accosted him as soon as the door had closed behind him.

"He's stubborn," Smith answered.

"He's a dangerous savage! Everybody believes that. If they didn't, they'd be in their own homes instead of barricaded here with us." Smith had not noticed a barricade.

"He must agree to honour the promises that brought us here." Mrs. Schultz seemed to have regained some of herself.

"My dear Mrs. Schultz," Smith began patiently, although his patience was beginning to wear out, "we must first agree to become part of Canada. If he decides to make his provisional government permanent—and he can—we are all finished here."

"Would you like some soup, Mr. Smith?" Mrs. Schultz interrupted. He was tired, dead tired. If he hadn't been, he would have heard Dr. Schultz's half-stated threat. "Some of us favour other ways of . . ." God! He wished he had heard it then.

Up the street from the Schultz house, in the Hudson's

Bay post, Louis continued to work on his plan long after Donald Smith had left. He sat at the old desk with the oil lamp burning above him while Gabriel slept soundly in the next room. Louis pondered the substance of his conversation with Smith. He wondered if he could trust him, or if he *should* trust him. How closely allied he was to the Canada Firsters Louis did not know. He knew only that Smith talked differently than the others and seemed to understand more about the Métis and their problems. And Smith was, after all, close to the Prime Minister. Perhaps the man was honest, perhaps he would speak in Ottawa for the provisional government and for the Métis.

Louis felt it imperative to finish working on more detailed points for further debate. A strange and exciting energy surged through him. He rose slowly and crossed the bare room to close the bedroom door. Gabriel was snoring and Louis found that the uneven but satisfying sounds distracted him. He worried that some of the Métis might not want the land they would have rights to, and he thought perhaps provisions for fair sale should be worked out. He turned himself to this task and was deep in thought.

Outside the window, on the far side of the office where he worked, Scott quietly loaded his rifle. "One well-placed shot should do it," he said to himself. He took aim and fired. Almost as soon as the bullet had left the barrel, Scott was on his way back to the Schultz house, approaching it quickly but by an indirect route. He entered it silently through the root cellar, which had its entrance in the back yard, but which emerged into the Schultz pantry.

Scott's bullet hit the oil lamp just above Louis' head, and as it came crashing down the explosion rocked the room and knocked Louis to the floor. Flames quickly engulfed the papers on the desk and began to spread. At that moment Gabriel Dumont threw open the door and dragged Louis' unconscious body away from the flames. Then he turned to fight the ever-growing blaze. Within minutes, he was joined by Goulet and Tremblay and together they finally managed to stamp out the fire.

Dumont ran to Louis. He held his seemingly lifeless body in his arms and let out a great cry. It seemed an eternity, but Louis finally opened his eyes. He was dazed but unhurt.

Gabriel, half in relief, half in anger, shouted, "Why do I listen to you?" Louis felt the affection in the otherwise angry question and he tried to smile at Dumont.

Gabriel shook his head and answered his own question. "Because you're one crazy fool—and I'm another."

Smith awoke to find Schultz and Scott packing hastily in the front room. Everyone was up and talking wildly. For one thing, nobody knew how Scott had gotten back to the house. It took Smith, who was groggy with sleep, a few minutes to piece it all together.

From the window someone yelled, "A single Métis rider is leaving the fort!"

"That's all?" asked Mrs. Schultz. She sank into a chair, dejected, and looked at Scott. "He's still alive! Otherwise they'd be all over us by now!"

Smith looked at the lot of them. He found he took great pleasure in his next statement. "They're hunters. They know where the quarry is . . . why waste shots in the dark? In a few hours there'll be enough light for them to calmly blow us to Kingdom Come." His eyes swept the room and came to rest on Scott. "You damn fool!"

Scott looked up at Smith. "You know something, mister? I don't trust you any more than I trust those half-breeds. What do you think of that?"

Smith did not deign to reply. At that moment he could have killed the ignorant sonofabitch with his bare hands. If Canada lost half a continent, the blame would eventually have to rest on this hot-headed numbskull. He wondered how history would write that up.

By the time the sun came up, two hundred Métis horsemen were in the square and a large black cannon was aimed directly at the front door of the Schultz house.

Gabriel Dumont was good-naturedly shooting the eaves off the house one by one when Riel rode up.

"You all right, Louis?"

Riel nodded and looked around.

"I wasn't sure what you wanted," Dumont laughed. "It gave the men something to do, eh? You gonna talk first, right?"

Riel nodded again. Dumont was grinning from ear to ear. "Maybe we be lucky and they won't hear you." Dumont gestured to the men to settle down. Isidore had the taper. He had always wanted to fire an *anglais* cannon.

Riel moved up and dismounted, while Dumont pointed his gun at the house.

"You inside! Are all of you so fearful of God's hand in judgment? Are your thoughts and actions unable to stand the test of even your own laws?" Louis' voice was loud and clear. "Are there none of you who will face us as equals?" Louis was shaking. He had been praying since before dawn. Why would they not recognize the Métis as equals? Hadn't he proved . . .

Dumont stepped forward, and with a bellow that could have been heard above the thunder of a thousand buffalo, shouted,

"You have one minute to come out or we'll blow you out! Do you hear me? This is Gabriel Dumont!"

The seconds passed.

"You have thirty seconds!" Dumont's voice rang through the square.

At ten seconds to go, one of the women came out first, carrying a baby in her arms. Slowly following her, the rest filed out one by one.

"I want no one hurt!" Riel addressed himself to the Métis.

Donald Smith followed MacAndrews out. He was surprised when he realized that Dr. Schultz, Scott, and Mrs. Schultz had not yet come out. Riel eyed the huddled group and approached the house.

Suddenly Mrs. Schultz strode out of the house and right up to Riel. It happened so suddenly that Smith was stunned. She was holding a gun to Louis' head.

"If anyone moves, I'll kill him!"

Everyone seemed to stop, frozen into position by this turn of events. Then Smith realized what had happened. Scott and Schultz had gone out the back, through the door in the pantry. No one moved to follow their fleeing horses as Mrs. Schultz held the gun to Riel's head. She looked none too steady and Smith hoped she would pass out.

It seemed to take an eternity for Scott and Schultz to ride through the open gate low in their saddles, and as they disappeared, Mrs. Schultz allowed her eyes to follow her husband and her lover.

Napoleon Nault was nearest.

Quickly he dove for her, knocking the gun out of her hand. She was pulled to her feet at the same time as twenty horsemen took off after the culprits.

Riel seemed quite calm. "Put them all under arrest." Smith started to walk away. "Mr. Smith, if you please." Smith looked up, puzzled. "Him too," Riel directed.

The Fort Garry jail would not have been ideal under any conditions, but now it was intolerable. The women had been placed in one cell, although the young mother and her baby had been sent home.

The men occupied the other filthy cell. For two days they dined on water, dried buffalo meat, and dark, hard bread. All that Smith could say for the whole experience was that Scott and Schultz were not there to listen to, and Mrs. Schultz was for once in her life reasonably quiet.

Now Riel sent for the Prime Minister's envoy. He

looked at Riel and decided to make his plea straight-away. "You can't keep these people here . . ."

Riel walked to the door and looked down the passage at the cells. "They choose to act like criminals—we respect their choice and treat them accordingly." Smith could not entirely disagree. "And then what?" Riel picked up the penknife on the desk and began tapping it in the palm of his hand. "They choose to believe we are savages, so, perhaps we scalp them. Or better yet, put on war paint and burn them at the stake."

Smith knew that Riel was not serious. Still, he was certainly serious in his intent, if not in his actual words and threats.

"Don't be unreasonable," he said.

Riel turned on him. "For God's sake, I have been far too reasonable, Mr. Smith. You see us as children requiring your benevolence to organize a government. If you persist in believing that . . . you and your friends here are all fools!"

Riel started to leave but Smith spoke calmly. "Release these people and let me present the facts to the Prime Minister."

Riel looked tired. "Father Ritchot tried. Your Prime Minister won't see him."

"I can change that, I give you my word," said Smith. He had not seen Dumont in the doorway and the sound of his voice caused him to turn sharply.

"The word of a politician? *Merde*!"

Dumont had reason to be suspicious. "No, Mr. Dumont. My word as a human being."

Louis said flatly, "You'll leave in the morning."

"And the prisoners?" Smith asked.

"I'll release Mrs. Schultz and the rest of them when you've left, but I won't let them gather in groups. They'll have to stay home and abide by the law."

"Agreed," he answered.

At dawn he left, as planned. About five miles from the border a grubby, unwashed creature ran in front of

96

his sleigh. Obviously Dr. Schultz was not a man accustomed to surviving in the bush. The Métis had probably not followed him too far because they knew he had nowhere to go.

"Where's Scott?" Smith asked.

"I don't know. We split up."

"Well, get under the blanket," Smith said curtly. "And stay there!" He had had quite enough of the "good" Dr. Schultz.

Now that Schultz was under the blanket, a giant tortoise with a great plaid shell, Smith did not know whether he felt a failure or a success. He knew that the situation was like a snowball running downhill—it began small, gathered endless amounts of snow, and was now bouncing off rocks at the bottom of some imaginary mountain of misunderstanding. Well, the Prime Minister was a pragmatic man, and he was glad. This situation demanded pragmatism at the very least. He could not imagine what could go wrong next and it was just as well that he couldn't.

Dumont finally called off the search for Scott. Schultz, he was sure, would head back to Ottawa. "These *anglais* settlers," he said to Goulet, "they're no good. You can't settle a land you don't know how to survive on." If Schultz had not headed for the U.S. border he was a fool, he thought. The man had no idea how to live in the bush, never mind that it was now winter.

Scott was different. Scott did know how to survive. The man was a rattlesnake, fast and dangerous. So, he and Goulet waited, unseen, unheard. If Scott came back, Dumont knew just where to find him.

It was close to midnight on the third night of their vigil. A solitary figure slipped furtively behind the Schultz house, paused, and then entered the house through the root cellar door. "Now?" Goulet whispered. "Nah," said Gabriel with a wicked smile. "Let him get his clothes off first and settle down." Goulet looked at

Dumont and returned his smile. "You one wicked bastard, Gabriel."

"A little justice for our *anglais* friends, just a little justice." The lights went on upstairs in Mrs. Schultz's bedroom, then after a while they went out again. "Now," said Gabriel.

They entered the house as Scott had and stole silently up the stairs. Neither of them seemed to be breathing as they paused outside the door.

From inside, Mrs. Schultz could be heard moaning, and there was thrashing on the bed. Dumont waited until the right moment, then flung the door open. In an instant he had pulled Scott off Mrs. Schultz and pinned him to the floor. Mrs. Schultz screamed and pulled the covers over her naked body. Goulet lit the lamp on the table and grinned.

"Savages! Savages!" she screamed. For once, Scott looked terrified. Dumont had one of his enormous hands on his throat, while the other held a gun firmly to his head. "Prairie dog always comes back to his own smell," said Dumont.

They left Mrs. Schultz screaming and dragged Scott down the stairs, out of the house, and up the street to the Hudson's Bay post. They threw him in the door and onto the floor. He looked up into the eyes of six Métis. All had their guns drawn.

"Better put these on," Goulet threw his pants to him as Riel entered the room.

"You bastard!" Scott muttered. Dumont laughed— Scott's nastiness seemed to have returned the moment he put his pants on. Maybe the *anglais* were nicer without their clothes.

Riel looked unmoved and undisturbed. "These men would kill you if I let them," he said.

Scott shuddered slightly, but he was slowly regaining himself.

"Let him taste justice instead," he added.

"Louis," Dumont said, looking Riel in the eye, "Métis

law, the law of the hunt. Our people understand that. Any other way . . ."

Louis shook his head. "Scott expects that, they all expect that. We must use Canadian justice, trial by jury, we must prove to them that we understand their system."

Dumont was disappointed. He knew Louis was not going to allow them to load Scott naked onto a horse and send him out onto the prairie. But he said no more. They took Scott to the Fort Garry jail and assigned four Métis to guard him.

The Council selected a jury of twelve, and the next morning the trial began. It was held in the small courtroom adjacent to the jail. Dumont testified that Scott had tried to kill Louis, and Scott's beating of young Napoleon Nault was also brought in as evidence against him.

Maxime Lépine served as judge. He listened intently to all the evidence. The Canadians refused to attend the trial. They would not testify either in Scott's favour or against him. The jury, headed by old Moise Ouellette, did not deliberate long, and Scott's guilt seemed evident to everyone.

Ouellette rose and began. "If we understand right, then this man, Tom Scott, he's guilty of going against our government here. The word for that is treason."

There was silence. Everyone's eyes were fixed on Tom Scott's face, even as old Ouellette continued.

"And from what I been told of those laws, people who are guilty of treason . . . we got to execute them."

Scott's face went white when he heard this pronouncement. "You're out of your bloody heads, you hear me! You stupid savages! I'm a British subject!"

"This isn't Britain!" Goulet shouted. Damned fool *anglais* didn't even know where he was!

Scott, now under sentence of death, was dragged back to the Fort Garry jail.

Riel returned to his office in the Hudson's Bay post. "Work," he thought. "There is so much to do."

He was drawing up detailed plans for the territory, points for negotiation, things he and Smith and the Council would have to thrash out.

It might have been two or three hours later. It was dark outside, and Louis suddenly felt very tired. The door abruptly opened and Mrs. Schultz stood before him.

"Your sense of timing is once again inappropriate, Mrs. Schultz," he said coldly.

"So is yours, Mr. Riel. Even more, you are presumptuous and impolite. May I at least be invited in?"

Louis motioned her into the room. She paused and then, suddenly more pleasant than he had ever seen her, she said, "That wasn't the way I had hoped to begin this conversation." Louis looked at her silently, but let her continue. He knew why she was there.

"You're still convinced we don't understand you. I think you don't understand us."

Now she wants understanding Louis thought. His eyes narrowed; he could not resist. "I understand about you and Scott."

Mrs. Schultz pulled herself up indignantly. "Mr. Riel, I'm not here to plead for a lover, though he was hardly that. A little diversion, perhaps, but Tom Scott a lover?" She shook her head.

Louis thought he could have developed a small particle of respect for the woman if she had loved Scott, if she had come to plead for him. "I'm not here to listen to a confession," he said. "I'm not a priest."

She leaned over and looked him squarely in the eye. "Us, Mr. Riel. The English. I am here as an English subject, and I tell you, if you think this act of violence will frighten us into kneeling to your demands, you, Mr. Riel, do not understand the English."

"We tried him under English law," Riel replied flatly.

"If you want to share our law with us, you must understand that law." She was insistent, and Louis thought, boring.

"I understand that law, Mrs. Schultz. I studied law in Quebec."

But she was not to be so easily silenced, or silenced at all, Louis suspected. She ignored his statement and continued.

"But you do not understand English justice. You proved your point when you found him guilty. You only prove ours if you insist on execution."

Riel stood up. She would not leave, so he would have to. "I must go, Mrs. Schultz."

"I too must go—to Ottawa, Mr. Riel. I must go to my husband."

Louis looked at her, thinking it was about time she thought of her husband. She must have understood his expression.

"Marriage is an unnatural state, Mr. Riel." Ah, thought Louis, a little philosophy from Mrs. Schultz. Naturally, she had more to say. "We are the only species of God's creation that insists on such confinement. Without compassion, without recognizing one another's needs, that state can become imprisonment. If your people and mine are destined to that kind of marriage, may God have mercy on us!" She swept out of the room and Louis sank back into his chair, thoroughly relieved.

He wondered how this woman could so easily invoke the name of God, could call on Him to justify her own petty desires and wishes. Mrs. Schultz's God was a very personal God indeed.

That night Louis went to the church. He prayed for many hours, gave thanks, and sought God's wisdom. To help the oppressed, to feed the hungry, to house the poor, to heal the sick—this was God's work. God would help him achieve his goals. His heart opened to all of them—the Métis, the Indians, even the English. There was time, there was land enough and will enough. God would show him the way.

The sun rose on a frozen prairie, rolling hills of white stretching away as far as the eye could see. The courtyard of the fort was bleak in the early morning light. A lonely cannon faced east. Two flags fluttered on the flagpole. Horses, tied to a nearby hitching rail, huddled together and nodded their great heads, nickering, seemingly in conversation. Two Métis guarded the gates while others stood in a group and checked the guns. Tom Scott, pale and shaking, was dragged from the jail, quickly hustled outside the fort, and tied to a post.

A few Canadians stood huddled together. Charles Mair was pulling Dumont's sleeve. "Stop them, Dumont . . . for God's sake."

"Métis law is simple. For such an offence we would send a man onto the plains alone. No horse, no gun. If God wants him to survive, he will survive. But if you don't know the Métis, how can you know our law? This," he continued, "is your law."

"Ready," Goulet's voice rang out. Everyone stiffened.

"Aim." Breathing seemed to cease.

"Fire!"

The rifles cracked in unison and the sound echoed all around the walls and out across the prairie. Scott's body crumpled. Riel stepped to the dying man's side. "I forgive you, Thomas Scott, for your sins and we will meet again in heaven where our Holy Father will make us one. I commend your soul to Almighty God." Louis made the sign of the cross and closed his eyes, his face filled with pain.

Goulet stepped forward, and placing his gun to Scott's head, fired the final merciful shot. Scott tumbled on his side. It was a shot that would be heard for thousands of miles, and for years afterward.

11

The Best-laid Plans . . .

*Alternatives, and particularly desirable alternatives,
grow only on imaginary trees.*

Saul Bellow

"Where's Father Ritchot?" Donald Smith asked Sir John A. Macdonald. Sir John was shaving in the small room adjacent to his office. He reached for a towel and eyed his old friend with interest.

"He's in Montreal, with Bishop Bourget."

"You didn't see him then?" Smith queried.

"I saw him in Montreal," Sir John replied.

"To what end?"

Sir John straightened his collar and pulled his dark jacket down neatly. "To find out what Riel had demanded, of course."

"And did you accept the demands?" Smith was not quite sure what had happened in his absence. Parliament was now in recess and Sir John was more relaxed.

"No," the Prime Minister replied, "I simply told him the climate would be warmer in Ottawa when you returned."

"It's good you did not reject them outright."

The Prime Minister's face remained unchanged. "Well, tell me about it, Donald. Tell me what this Riel really wants."

"There's not a damn thing he wants that you wouldn't offer him anyway. Give him a way to fit into Confederation, a way that he can live with, and you have the railroad and the West! Riel wants to be part of Canada, Sir John!"

"How comforting," the Prime Minister commented. "How very comforting." Sir John moved to his desk and withdrew a letter from his top drawer. "It came early this morning, by dispatch."

Smith unfolded it and read the message. The printed words seemed to move beneath his vision. He couldn't say he was surprised. He couldn't even say he was sorry. He only wished it had not happened.

"They shot Scott." When he said it out loud, it sounded even worse than it looked on paper. Smith sat down in the leather chair facing the Prime Minister. His body sank into the deep leather and the weariness of the past weeks swept over him. He was tired, oh so very tired.

Strangely, the Prime Minister seemed quite calm. He was a man who firmly believed, on the basis of all past experience, that if something could go wrong, it would go wrong—and it had!

After a few moments of reflection, Smith said evenly, "We can't just knock Dumont and Riel out of Fort Garry. No matter what happened to Scott, or why, reality is still reality. Their government is perfectly legal."

The Prime Minister stroked his chin. "Nor can we simply give in, Donald."

Smith noticed a glint in the Prime Minister's eye. He wondered if he had a plan. He wasn't sure he even wanted to know what it was.

"It's December, Donald. Can't do much until spring. You're right, though. We do have to do a little something now."

Smith was relieved, but he knew the Prime Minister must have something in mind. Sir John would know what Scott's death could mean to the rest of the country.

"Send for Father Ritchot, Donald. Pry him from the hold of our friend, Bishop Bourget."

It took two days for Father Ritchot to return from Montreal, and in those two days the news of Scott's death swept the province of Ontario. His name was praised in every Orangeman's hall. Naturally his trial and conviction meant nothing—he had been "murdered" by the Papist half-breeds.

Father Ritchot was due at two o'clock in the Prime Minister's office. Donald Smith was expected as well.

The latter had the carriage driver stop as soon as they crossed the Rideau Canal. Walking, even through the snow, would clearly be easier and perhaps safer, he thought. He pulled his coat around him and lifted his collar, then wrapped his scarf under his nose. His heavy clothing now covered his famous beard, effectively disguising him. It was a good day to be anonymous.

The crowds swarmed around the East block but they were held twenty feet away by armed guards, whose black capes whipped in the winter wind and whose tall fur hats gave them the appearance of being much taller than they actually were. If the faces of the protesters had not been filled with such hate, and if the signs they carried had not been so venomous, the whole scene could have been mistaken for a carnival. A band played patriotic music, an old man sold roasted chestnuts from an ancient cart, and bright orange banners and Union Jacks were being waved by nearly everyone.

"Murderer! Riel is a murderer! Down with Macdonald! Avenge Tom Scott!" the crowd chanted.

Smith recognized Dr. Schultz and that fellow Evans, before they saw him. He ducked and took a path that made a wide sweep around the East block and terminated at the rear exit of the building.

Father Ritchot was a small man. He sat on the edge of Macdonald's great leather chair in order not to sink into it. He was a shepherd anxious to return to his flock—Ottawa was definitely not for him and Montreal was too big, too disturbing. Was the church divided? He did not know, or care. What were these ecclesiastical struggles to him? He was just a poor country priest. What, he asked himself, was he doing here in the Prime Minister's office?

Sir John A. Macdonald held out the brown envelope with the official seal of his office embossed on it. "You may tell Mr. Riel that, as he wishes, this new province shall be called Manitoba, and that a new governor will be sent out in the spring. Provincial elections will take place at that time." The Prime Minister reached out and shook the hand of Father Ritchot and continued. "I hope that this measure will receive the acceptance of the people of the Red River."

Father Ritchot cleared his throat and glanced for reassurance at Donald Smith, who stood to the Prime Minister's right.

"Mr. Prime Minister, there is now . . ." he paused, and gestured to the noise below, "there is now the question of amnesty."

The Prime Minister looked weary with the question. "We will not be prosecuting any members of the provisional government. We could hardly prosecute the members of a government we choose to accept for three months as the legal provisional government."

Time, Macdonald thought to himself, time.

Father Ritchot was beaming broadly. Perhaps he would not make too bad a diplomat, he thought. "Thank you," he said.

"Better see my secretary, Father." The Prime Minister still seemed quite serious, considering the deed was done. "He will arrange for the guards to spirit you out of the building, and Ottawa and Ontario for that matter."

"I am grateful," Father Ritchot replied.

"It would not do for a priest to be hit with an egg," Macdonald said, a little sarcastically. Father Ritchot left quietly, thinking only that the Prime Minister was a strange man. Yes, a very strange man.

Sir John moved to the window.

"It's a small group," Smith said, dismissing the crowd.

The Prime Minister sighed. "Small groups, when they're loud, have a way of getting bigger." He leaned forward and peered down at the crowd. "Is that Schultz there?"

"Yes. He's at the centre of it."

"Those people out there can represent a thousand votes . . . who knows, ten thousand."

"You've just made a commitment here, remember?" Smith said it because he knew what the Prime Minister was thinking. Just for good measure he added, ". . . to the railway. You made a commitment to our railway."

The Prime Minister turned to face him, his hand in his watch pocket. "Donald, you're blessed by being a businessman. Your life is guided by a single force—money. Bishop Bourget's life is guided by two forces—the church and the French language. I am cursed by being a politician. A businessman is immune to love, a Bishop inherits it with his mantle, and a politician seeks it from his people by doing what he believes is right and trusting the factions he governs will understand. My life—this country—is plagued by factions. There are too many . . . symbols! Now Thomas Scott and Louis Riel are symbols—the English Protestant and the French Catholic, the easterner and the westerner, the white man and the half-breed. The span of a man's life is brief, Donald, but symbols have a way of living for a long time . . ."

The winter months passed uneventfully in the province now called Manitoba. All factions were silenced for the time being—the winter was very hard and politics, animosities, and struggles with the government gave way to the struggle for survival. Louis worked away at his plans and spent much of his time in contemplation and prayer. God had directed his actions—his people would have their land.

Sir John A. Macdonald walked from the House to the East block. The cold damp winds of early March swept across the expanse of snow and clouds of tiny white particles danced about his head. Donald Smith walked next to him, hands in the pockets of his coat. Looking about him it was hard to believe that in a few weeks the snow would be gone and long-buried grass would blanket the Parliamentary lawns in green rather than white. Neither of them spoke until they entered the Prime Minister's chambers.

"A drink, Donald?" The Prime Minister extended a glass of scotch.

"Just a little to take out the chill."

"Well, it's done," Sir John said. "Manitoba is an official province."

"And when will Governor Archibald leave?" Smith queried.

"I imagine around the first, or maybe the middle of April."

Smith was stunned. "April! Why so late, why not next week?"

The Prime Minister smiled. "Because General Wolseley can't have his peacekeeping troops there until at least the . . ."

"Troops!" Smith blurted out, truly astounded by what he had heard. "You don't need troops!"

"I *do* need them, Donald." The Prime Minister turned and was looking out the window.

"The Americans won't let you, I'm sure they wouldn't."

"Quite right, Donald. They wouldn't. That fellow Seward was barely civil. Bloody American imperialist!"

Smith's mind buzzed. "You can't be going to send them overland!"

"I am and I will. They leave day after tomorrow."

"It's never been done. I don't think it can be done." Smith himself had made the trip several times, of course, and even in summer it was a misery. One had to be a first-class woodsman. To send an army was madness.

"It has to be done." The Prime Minister was glaring at him now very intently. "The Americans will forever covet our West unless we secure it. We have to show them we can reach it, occupy it, and govern it."

"Without the railway . . ." Smith did not finish his sentence. He could see that Sir John would do as he planned. He also knew that the Prime Minister was right about the Americans. They would see it as a weakness that Canada could not even reach her own territory with an army. The Irish were always agitating with the Americans, and some Métis even favoured the Americans. With a sigh he realized that Sir John was right. Still, he wondered about the Métis.

"You'll keep your promises to Riel?" he asked.

"Yes. We have no intention of prosecuting."

"Sir John." Smith knew he sounded demanding. "General Wolseley's command, his troops, are primarily from Ontario and a lot of them are probably Orangemen. They'll want Riel, and they won't understand the Métis."

Sir John looked annoyed. "General Wolseley is an excellent general. I'm sure he can control twelve hundred men."

Only, Smith thought, if he knows what they are doing, *and* if he disagrees with them.

The military expedition began all wrong, just as Donald Smith had feared.

There was a celebration of leavetaking by the troops, the magnitude of which Smith had not believed possible. The railway stations were packed with orange banners and marching bands, mothers kissing their sons, and sweethearts their lovers. The peacekeeping force clearly thought it was off to put down a violent rebellion by Indians and Frenchmen and nothing could quiet the rumours or stop the talk.

Once on their way, the more miserable the trip got, the more hatred the soldiers built up for Riel and the "rebels." And the trip *was* misery. Ninety-six days of cold and mud, of frostbite and agony, insects and stifling heat. First there were the mosquitos—they were everywhere and hungry for blood. The days were warm enough by the end of April for the flies to be bothersome, those flies that stung and bit and pestered the men ceaselessly. The melting snow often turned the rivers and streams into raging torrents and the ground was always cold, wet and soggy. Men got wet all day and then froze in the still cool nights. They bound their swollen feet, but the bindings got soaked in mud. Few, if any, had sufficient clothing, tents, or food for such a journey. As they plodded along, dysentery swept the ranks, fevers were common, and some even suffered from poison ivy. They lay in their soaked clothes freezing at night, dreaming of the revenge they would take.

"Will we string the bastard half-breed up when we catch his yellow hide?" Another yelled, "Kill the papists! Dirty half-breeds!"

The talk around the camps did not bode well for the Métis. Smith prayed that Sir John had been right and that Wolseley could control his men. At least he was happy about the new governor, Adams G. Archibald. He was a fair and generous man, a man who would keep his word.

Whispering Pines rode silently through the night. He had watched the fires of the soldiers for weeks now. He crept as close as he could to the fires and listened to everything, memorizing the words he heard spoken in the night air.

Whispering Pines wondered what kind of women these white braves had. When his braves were travelling, the women prepared everything, but these men had nothing —their squaws must have been heartless creatures to allow such a thing.

One afternoon he watched the soldiers fording a rocky river. It was spring, and the waters ran rapidly and high. They were cold with melting snow and ice upstream. He watched as the soldiers dragged themselves through the mud on both shores, sinking in as far as a man could and still move. The mud was cold and it stuck to them. Some of the soldiers, he noted, could hardly walk. Their white man's boots were not for this country. He watched them eat too, and knew the food was not enough. White men all feared death. It was something Whispering Pines had observed. No wonder, he thought, none of them knew how to live. If they had scouted, they would have found a crossing upstream. It could have saved much time and much mud.

Whispering Pines stayed with the soldiers another week and then turned his horse and rode west on one of the trails he knew. No soldier could follow him. When he reached the village of his brothers he passed on his information, and another rider set out in a westerly direction. The information was passed from mouth to mouth, from rider to rider, until an Ojibway named Great Bear approached Gabriel Dumont in Fort Garry and spoke with him at great length.

Riel was in prayer. His eyes scanned the paintings on the walls of the church. He saw Moses giving the Commandments to his people. God's leader he thought . . . out of the wilderness, he took his people out of the wilderness. And David, David the king, David who slew the giant, Goliath. His eyes came to rest on the Christ. Tears ran down his face and his body shook. "Take my hand, God. Lead me, help me lead my people . . . my destiny, my dest—"

"Louis!" the voice crackled, and the silence of the church was destroyed. Louis, tears still streaming down his face, looked up into the eyes of Gabriel Dumont.

"You are the avenging angel," Louis said.

Dumont's face showed his dismay. His beard was longer, for he had been out hunting for over a week, and his eyes were wild. At that moment he looked more like an Indian than a Frenchman.

"Louis! We must go. You, me, Goulet, Lépine, the others. The Canadians are sending troops overland, and those troops they want the hides of Louis Riel and Gabriel Dumont!"

Louis was stunned, but he stood up and silently followed Gabriel out of the church. His mind was filled with hows and whys.

"You talk to God later!" Gabriel said, as they mounted the two fresh horses that Lépine and the others had brought. "Right now, you come with me!"

"How much farther?" Julie Riel called out to her travelling companion, Napoleon Nault.

"We are soon there," he hollered cheerfully.

Julie's long hair was again in braids and today she dressed as a Cree woman might. They had been riding since early morning and she was stiff and sore. Normally she took the wagon—this was the first time she had ridden in several years. Napoleon too had discarded his Métis clothes. His light hair had been dyed black by the Cree women and his fair skin had been rubbed with berry juice that turned it darker. Somewhere ahead of them were Madeleine, Dumont's wife, old Ouellette, and the girl they called Marie. The three of them travelled in a Red River cart with what belongings they had left.

Napoleon brought his horse closer to Julie now. "It's all right," he said. "We are no longer in Canada." She smiled across at him and they rode their horses more slowly side by side. "Are you very tired?" he inquired. "Should we go to Pembina so you can rest?"

She shook her head. "No, let us go directly to Louis and the others. I'll rest when we are together."

"I'm glad you have come," Napoleon said. "Louis will stop worrying now. You will calm him."

Julie felt a terrible sadness, an emptiness—and fear. "He will comfort me," she said simply.

They rode together silently for two more hours and as they approached a cluster of rough log cabins, Julie did not see the Métis guards who had watched for them for so long, but she saw the wagon. Good! The others had also arrived without incident.

Louis flung open the door and ran out to greet his mother. She dismounted and they melted into one another's arms.

"I'm all right Louis," she said, "I'm fine. They did not hurt me."

Louis looked at her arms and saw the row of bruises. "What are these then?"

"Nothing," she whispered. "Nothing. I will tell you everything. Just let me sit down and rest for a while."

"Of course, mother. I am too quick. Forgive me, I have been so worried."

The fire crackled in the fireplace and they drank tea and ate brown bread together. Julie stared into the flames as she spoke. Madeleine held Gabriel's hand and Ouellette gently cradled Marie in his lap. Julie pulled a blanket about her; she was always cold and occasionally she coughed. It was nearly the first of June, but the nights were still cold.

"They are burning our homes and farms," she said at last. "They came looking for you, Louis."

"And the bruises?" he asked.

"They destroyed the furniture, broke all the lamps, and then they began chopping up the bed and burning the covers. I couldn't stand it. I attacked them and they threw me to the floor."

Tears filled Louis' eyes. He knew how his mother had loved her oak bed—it was her prize possession, the symbol of the past with his father. "I have brought you this sadness—it is my doing."

"No, no." She too was crying. "You did what you had to. The English bring me sadness."

"And our house?" Gabriel asked Madeleine.

"Yes. They destroyed everything. They are like a swarm of locusts over the prairie. They destroy everything, they eat what is in their way and spit it out in the faces of the Métis." Madeleine stood up and pointed to the sleeping child. "Look at her, she is not yet a woman, but she is now more than a child." Madeleine's voice was filled with passion. "They killed her parents and burned her home. They left her in the hay when they had finished with her body . . . *Crisse*! She is only ten years old! What animals are these *anglais*!"

Madeleine collapsed against Gabriel, whose eyes were filled with hatred. He knew what language the soldiers understood. "When did we ever burn their homes, rape their women, or destroy their farms! *Maudits Canadiens*! Let me fight them, Louis! We should have attacked them as they approached! They were tired then!"

Louis closed his eyes. He felt a terrible responsibility and a strong sense of the failure of his mission.

Julie stroked his hand. "You have done everything, Louis. No one blames you—quite the contrary."

"What do you mean?" he asked. "How can they not blame me?"

"They do not, we do not," Madeleine said. "The elections are soon. Your name, the name of Louis Riel, is everywhere."

"It is true," old Ouellette chimed in. "It is true."

"Everywhere are posters with your name. They tear them down and the Métis put up more. They write with dye on the buildings," Napoleon said excitedly.

"They write?" Louis asked.

"Yes," Napoleon replied, "they can write nothing else but the name of Louis Riel. They *can* write 'Louis Riel.' "

Louis began to feel better, but guilt still plagued him.

Where had he gone wrong? Why had they not respected their own laws? He should never have trusted them!

The days passed quickly in their hideaway just across the U.S. border. Madeleine and Julie cooked the wild rabbit the men hunted, and sometimes they killed a chicken from the roost that lay behind their huddle of small cabins. It had once been a lumber camp, they learned, but now it was abandoned. James Wickes Taylor, the American, had arranged their temporary exile and he had provided them with the chickens and occasionally some wine. Life was not bad there, but it was temporary, it was not their home.

Marie seemed to get better as the weeks passed and the sun warmed the days. She talked with Madeleine and Julie and they instructed her on sewing and on gathering faggots for the evening fire. At night, old Ouellette told her stories of the buffalo hunts and chilling tales from the lore of the Cree and the Blackfoot. Ouellette was nearly eighty, and little Marie reminded him of his granddaughter.

"The young need the old," Gabriel had said. "It is part of our life, the youngest learn from the old ones, not from their parents."

Riel spent much of his time walking. Sometimes he prayed at the altar he had built near the cabins, repeating biblical phrases to himself. Christ had taken the sins of the world on Himself, and the weight of his own guilt was heavy. The light of the candles flickered as they burned down. Madeleine had drifted off to sleep, Julie had gone to bed in another cabin, and little Marie huddled in her bedroll asleep in a corner. Louis sat at the table by the dying light of the candles, reading from his books while Gabriel stared out the window into the dark stillness of the night.

"You'll go blind, Louis. You read too much."

Louis looked up and closed his book slowly. "You are right, my friend, it is late. I hope God will forgive me," he continued. "I have not succeeded. Why can't they understand? Why can't I make them understand?"

"They don't want to understand. They want land."

"God will make them understand." Louis looked even paler than before. His eyes glistened in the flickering light and his dark hair was wild around his face. He looked haunted by his guilt, desperate with his failure.

Louis walked over to Gabriel. "God will make them understand, Gabriel!" Louis grasped Gabriel's arm. Dumont felt a power in Louis' grip. It was as though the full strength of his body flowed through his fingers. They tightened, and although Gabriel's arms were strong and muscular, he could feel the strength of the grip. "God will make them understand," he repeated.

Gabriel covered Louis' hand with his free hand and loosened his hold. "Yes, Louis," he said calmly. "Of course He will."

He was about to turn from the window when he heard the prearranged signal. He listened for the second call of the night bird and then said, "Two riders are coming."

"Friends?" Louis asked. He did not want to hear more stories of what the soldiers were doing; he couldn't bear to think of it.

"Yes, friends," answered Gabriel. "Friends."

The horses came fast now and Gabriel could hear the hooves beating on the prairie. He flung open the front door and silhouetted against the moon were two figures on horseback, riding hard. He squinted and tried to make them out. One was Pierre Nault, Napoleon's father, and the other was Father Ritchot. Gabriel heard their whoops from a distance. Something had happened, something good.

"We won! We won!" Pierre was not yet off his horse, but the others were coming out of their cabins. "We won! We won!" he hollered. "Louis Riel is a Member of Parliament!"

Gabriel laughed with relief and joy and turned to hug his friend in congratulation. He swept down in a mock bow. "Your Honour, I welcome you to the House of Parliament!" He stood up and looked into a different face. The eyes were no longer haunted, the old colour was there, and a smile broke across Louis' face. "Gabriel, you're coming with me to Ottawa!"

"Make me," Gabriel laughed, and they all laughed together.

But Father Ritchot stood silently. "I don't think you should go," he said warily.

"I must go," Louis replied. "I must go and have it out with them in Parliament. I can make them understand."

"The church will not approve," the priest said sadly.

"They will approve," Louis countered. "I do God's will. I always do God's will."

12

The Road to Madness

*Injustice in this world is not something comparative;
the wrong is deep, clear, and absolute in each private
fate.*

George Santayana

Gabriel Dumont stood in the courtyard and looked up.
He did not like Montreal. He sat down on the stone
bench and looked at the flowers in the Bishop's garden.
So trained, so straight, row upon row, he thought. Father
Charles McWilliams, Louis' friend from the seminary,
entered the garden quietly. McWilliams sat down next to
Dumont.

"I am Louis' friend too," he said simply. "When did
this all start?"

Gabriel shook his head. He wasn't really sure how to
answer.

"First," he began, "three of us started out for Ottawa.
Him, myself, and our brother, Elzéar Goulet." He
thought the tears would come to his eyes when he
thought of Goulet. He paused. "We rode a trail we
know . . . we thought it was in the U.S., maybe it's in
Canada, who knows?"

"He said something about Goulet," McWilliams
offered. "I couldn't understand."

"Some *anglais* soldiers," Gabriel continued, "they
were on the other side of the river Louis and I had

crossed. Goulet, he was about half-way. One of them shot him. He fell in the river and tried to swim. Riel, he go after Goulet, but it was no good."

"He died?" McWilliams asked quietly.

"Yeah, he die in Louis' arms. I shot all three of the . . . soldiers."

"And then you went to Ottawa, the two of you?"

"Yes." Gabriel smiled a little. The day in Ottawa was not one he would soon forget.

"I have to sign the official register," Louis said. He left Dumont near the great spiral staircase and walked straight up to the desk, turned the great book around, and signed his name. *Provencher: Louis Riel, M.P.* The clerk was busy and did not look up. Suddenly Dumont saw them—Dr. Schultz, Charles Mair, and a group of others.

He ran up to Louis. "The hunting party, they're here!"

"They can't do anything now! I'm officially registered."

"We'll write that on your tombstone—'Louis Riel, shot down in Parliament.' Officially registered! Dammit, we do this my way!"

He guided Louis through a nearby doorway, into a room full of books, and shoved him into a chair. "Don't move. Please don't move!"

Louis looked up without comprehension. "I'm not afraid of them!"

"*Be* afraid for God's sake! Write a speech, anything, just stay here for a few minutes . . ."

Gabriel looked out into the corridor cautiously and heard Schultz speaking to the Parliamentary clerk . . . "You idiot! How could you let him do it? How could you let him just walk in and sign?" Dumont saw that all four men had pistols.

Louis was still sitting when he returned. He looked at Gabriel with curiosity in his eyes.

"We're getting out of here!"

Louis did not move. "After I deliver my speech."

Gabriel grabbed him and pulled him roughly to his feet and behind a corridor of books. "Listen to me, Louis. They have guns! They mean to kill you! Do you understand, Louis? Kill you! *Before* you make your speech."

Louis blinked at him and yielded to his guiding arm. A woman at the desk was giving some books to a tall grey-haired man. He was lean, with hollow cheeks, grey sideburns, and thick unruly hair. Gabriel turned to Louis, who had a dazed expression on his face. "Not a word," he ordered. "Not one single word."

Gabriel tapped the grey-haired gentleman on the shoulder. "Excuse me, sir. Is there a way to the front door? We make one turn, two turns, and now we're lost."

The gentleman smiled and motioned to them. "Just go along the hall and down the stairs."

Gabriel purposely started off in the wrong direction.

"No no," the man said. "Here, let me show you." They started to walk together, three abreast. The gentleman looked at Louis. "Is your friend all right? He doesn't look well."

"He's fine," Gabriel answered. "Just overwhelmed by the greatness of what he has seen here."

They glided through a door, a great oak door that reached to the ceiling. "And where are you from?" the man inquired.

"Manitoba," Gabriel answered back, "Manitoba."

They ran out the door and Gabriel steered Louis toward a carriage. He looked back long enough to see Schultz and the others being restrained by the grey-haired man.

The driver looked back at them as they headed down Wellington. "Prime Minister give you a private tour, did he?"

That was the part Gabriel was going to remember.

(TOP) *Gabriel Dumont (right), the Métis general, in Buffalo Bill Cody's Wild West Show.*
(BOTTOM) *Dumont relates the end of the Métis dream of nationhood – and of his people's leader, Louis Riel.*

Louis Riel (left) and Gabriel Dumont — "the head" and "the heart" of the Métis people.

(TOP) *Thomas Scott (right) and his survey party encounter an angry group of Métis. Scott and his henchmen threaten the Métis party, but are themselves forced to retreat.* (BOTTOM) *The unarmed Métis stand their ground.*

(TOP) *Riel and his followers celebrate their capture of the Hudson's Bay Company post of Fort Garry.*
(BOTTOM) *Dumont and Riel establish the National Committee of the Métis of Red River.*

William McDougall, Sir John A. Macdonald's Governor-designate, is forcefully stopped from entering Fort Garry.

(TOP) *Bishop Bourget of Montreal (left) and Sir John A. Macdonald (right) meet at Montreal to discuss Riel and the events at Fort Garry.*

(BOTTOM) *At the fort, relations between the English faction and the Métis reach the boiling point. Here, Mrs. Schultz threatens Riel.*

The execution of Thomas Scott for the attempted murder of Riel.

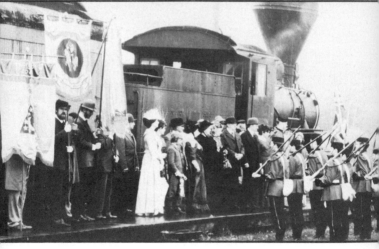

Canadian troops and militia depart for the Northwest.

Major Crozier and his Canadian troops are driven back at Duck Lake by Dumont and the Métis.

Louis Riel, prophet and martyr, prays for his cause and his people.

The battle for Batoche.

The cross in the wilderness — Riel exhorts his men to victory.

The Métis defeat at Batoche marks the end of the dream of nationhood.

The trial of Louis Riel, July, 1885.

Louis Riel is hanged for treason at Regina,
November 16, 1885.

Father McWilliams was listening intently. In spite of their mutual and deep concern for Louis, the story was not without irony. "You are a good protector," he said to Dumont.

Dumont returned McWilliams' look. "I have not done enough."

They were silent for a few minutes. "Is there more?" McWilliams asked at length.

"We came here," Gabriel answered. "We stopped one night, but we came here. Louis was in a dream. He kept saying, 'Take me to the Bishop, take me to the Bishop!'"

"It is good," McWilliams said. "It is good. I have given him something to make him sleep. He is resting now."

McWilliams took Dumont's hand. "Come, I will show you to a room. Tomorrow Louis can speak with the Bishop."

Gabriel felt distinctly uncomfortable in the small cell-like room. There was a narrow iron bed with a single mattress and stiff, starched white linen. Above it hung a large black crucifix and in one corner sat a small table with an oil lamp. On the table was a pencil, some paper, and a prayer book, and behind that a statue of the Virgin Mary, her heart exposed and bleeding.

Gabriel crossed himself as he always did in Father Ritchot's church. He discarded his clothes and got into bed. Only on his back could he be comfortable. The sheets slipped to the floor as he tossed, trying to find a comfortable position. A man was not meant to sleep like this he thought. He was meant to sleep under the stars.

"There is nothing you can do, my son." Bishop Ignace Bourget looked into the tired eyes of Louis Riel.

Louis protested. "The trial was legal, Your Grace. It was according to Canadian law . . . *their* law. The jury found him guilty. They must be made to understand. I killed no one, I could kill no one . . ." Louis sank into the deep red velvet chair and looked into the Bishop's eyes.

"You need rest, Louis. A safe haven."

"I want to go to Parliament, I want to take my seat! They must understand!" His fist came down on the Bishop's desk.

"They have revoked your seat," the Bishop said softly.

"They can't! They can't do that! I was elected by the people!" Louis seemed suddenly alert. His eyes began to shine with a mysterious energy as he addressed the Bishop. "You once told me you have a great love for our people."

"And I do," the Bishop replied.

"Then help me! In the name of God, help me make them understand!"

The Bishop tried to make contact with Louis' eyes. "I am. I am trying to help you, Louis. For your own sake, for your people's, for the church . . . listen to reason!"

Louis suddenly stood, his eyes flashing, and again the wavering energy returned. "I have been lied to, used, betrayed. I have watched one of my oldest friends die in my arms. Now I am called a criminal and pursued by men who would feel fully justified in killing me! You would have me listen to reason? Where is reason?" He paused to gather his thoughts. "There must be a way to get through to these people . . . to get what I promised the Métis . . . I will find that way!"

He reeled and went quickly out the door, his eyes blind with tears. "I will find that way," he muttered.

The Bishop turned to the silent McWilliams. "He cannot leave here like this."

McWilliams nodded. "He needs help. We must help him."

"Will you go to him now, Father McWilliams?"

"Not yet. It is time for mass. Perhaps he will come."

"Perhaps," the Bishop answered vaguely.

When he entered the chapel, McWilliams was not

surprised to see Dumont sitting in the back pew. He nodded and sat down beside him.

"Where's Louis? Did he talk to the Bishop?" Dumont whispered.

"Yes, but I don't know where he is. I think he will come here when the bells are rung."

Gradually the chapel filled with young clerics and novitiates. Above the chapel the bells pealed, and neither man was surprised when Louis slipped into the pew beside McWilliams and dropped to his knees, crossing himself. McWilliams could see only the pale profile, the fine straight nose, the dark brown hair. His eyes were closed. The moments passed and the familiar ritual continued. McWilliams glanced periodically at Louis, who was still deep in prayer.

The priest raised the chalice high above his head and intoned, *"Et spiritu sancti."*

Louis stiffened and sat up. McWilliams turned, but not in time. A smile covered Louis' face, and he radiated. A small laugh came from deep in his throat and then he started laughing hysterically. McWilliams tried to take his arm. "Louis, Louis, stop this!"

But Louis' eyes seemed glazed and he could not hear McWilliams.

"God has spoken to me! God has spoken to me!" he cried, shaking McWilliams, who felt the pain of his grip. His laughter ripped through the chapel and faces turned, eyes stared, horrified.

Louis grasped his temples as the stabbing pain once again cut through his whole body. He let out one long terrifying scream and fell to the floor, white foam covering his pale lips. "God has spoken to me." His voice gurgled from deep inside. "Rise up, Louis Riel! Through you all the children of the world shall be blessed!" His body became rigid and he went catatonic as if in death, his eyes peering blankly upward at the ceiling above.

The painted Virgin smiled benevolently down on him.

Louis' head throbbed, his body ached, and his vision was blurred. When he moved, his feet did not seem to touch the ground, and objects seemed to float before his bloodshot eyes. His arms hung lifelessly at his side. His body seemed uncontrollable, and as he was led along the corridor he felt he was looking down on himself, a spirit detached from his own physical presence.

The corridor was long and dimly lit, grey and damp, and eyes looked at him, followed him, pursued him. He vaguely noticed some huddled figures standing in doorways that lined the long corridor. One grinned at him as he passed and said, "My cakes are three shillings, do you want one?" But there were no cakes to be seen. The man's toothless grin faded and turned to anger. "Cheapskate!" he called after Louis and the strange arms that guided him through his nightmare. An old woman blocked their way. She was dressed in loose pajamas and her brown tangled hair tumbled down her back and stood out on all sides of a withered face. "I have a baby," she said proudly. "Do you want to see my baby?" Three others stood together and simply stared. One woman, quite young, slumped on the floor near a door and cried. Louis heard a terrible scream somewhere in the distance. He began to shake, for it seemed to him his nightmare had such substance, such reality. He shook his head—the aching seemed to have stopped.

The arm led him to a door. They stopped, the door was opened, and Louis found himself in a well-lighted room, a room which, after the long endless grey of the corridor and its strange inhabitants, seemed filled with colour and life. One wall of the room was lined with books, while from another hung neatly framed certificates. The man behind the great oak desk wore white, and his glasses rested on the end of his nose. He looked at Louis over the top of them as he was directed to a chair in front of the desk.

Louis waited and then asked warily, "What is this place? Who are you?"

The man smiled kindly, but he answered slowly as if he were addressing a child. "It is Longue Pointe Asylum, and my name is Dr. Roy. Your friends felt that your life might be in danger, and that you needed rest and help. This is an excellent place to hide." The doctor paused, ". . . and we can help you too."

Louis suddenly realized it was not a nightmare—it was real. The people in the corridor were mad. Was he mad too then? He couldn't remember anything except having been in mass. Then for a time he was in a room, writing, then some people came and tried to take him somewhere. He remembered a struggle and then nothing, nothing until the nightmarish trip down the grey corridor. "Asylum?" It was neither a question nor a statement. When he said it aloud, the word seemed real. "Where is my friend Gabriel Dumont?" What had happened? He couldn't put it together. It was a frightening thing to have a period of one's life forgotten, erased, gone. How long had it been? Hours? Days? Weeks? The doctor handed him some tea.

As he began to sip it he had a flash come to him. Yes, he had been working on a plan for the territory, a wonderful plan. He would make a home for all the oppressed peoples of the world there; it would be a haven for them. Refugees from oppression would settle the West and together with the Métis would build a nation of love and justice. Did this dream to open the West for settlement by refugees make him mad?

"What do you remember?" the doctor inquired gently.

Louis looked at him carefully. "I was writing . . . I had an idea . . . I . . ." He stopped. He was beginning to remember more. "Some priests came from Ottawa . . . they said I was to be exiled . . . I, I think I attacked them." Louis stopped again and looked at the doctor. "Yes. I hit them. Are they all right?"

"They are fine—you were just distraught."

Louis sank back into the chair. His body began to relax now, muscles which had been tense felt looser. "It was a foolish bit of anger. I hope they will forgive me."

The doctor rose from his chair. "You were quite disturbed, Mr. Riel."

Louis pulled himself up, suddenly feeling very sleepy, but also calmer than he had before, and stronger. "Well, I'm all right now . . . If you'll have my things returned, I'd like to leave." Louis drained his teacup and looked at the residue of leaves in the bottom.

The doctor looked at him with concern. "But you have been admitted here! Under another name, of course —simply Louis David."

Louis felt suddenly defeated. "Admitted?" There was disbelief in his voice.

"As a patient. Your friends feel that you've become, well, *strained*. The mind, like the body, Mr. Riel . . ." The doctor paused. "May I call you Louis?" Louis nodded, and the doctor continued, ". . . can become overtired. Sometimes the mind needs rest, time to clarify reality."

Louis leaned forward. "I have so much to do . . ."

The doctor nodded. "Tell me about that, tell me about your visions."

"I have a mission, Dr. Roy, to return to the West."

"Is it a holy mission?" the doctor asked.

Louis chose his words carefully. "I believe that God directs me."

The doctor turned to look out the window. "God 'directs' you, is that correct?"

"I have prayed, I have listened." Louis paused. "I heard the voice of God."

The doctor turned and confronted Louis. "And the voice of God said that you are a saviour to your people . . . a messiah?"

"There is only one Saviour, one Messiah." Louis was

weary, tired of trying to explain. "I don't expect you to understand."

"But I do understand, Louis. Sometimes people . . ."

"What are you saying, Doctor?"

Dr. Roy spoke evenly, slowly, deliberately. "I am saying that sometimes people who have visions and hear voices, and who put themselves in danger, sometimes those people need to be helped."

Louis felt dizzy. His eyes were unable to focus properly. He looked into the teacup again. "What have you given me?" he moaned.

"Just a little sedative we use here . . . to calm you. To begin helping you."

Louis felt he might pass out. He did not need a sedative, he'd just begun to remember, to come out of his dream.

"We'll talk again in a few days. Please, rest now."

Louis hardly heard the doctor's last words. The arm began to lead him again, out the door and down that long grey nightmare of a corridor.

A day, two days, a month. Louis did not know. Food was brought, medicine was given, and he and Dr. Roy talked. The place was a horror to him. Its inmates were filled with their own private terrors, their own dreams, their own nightmares. Ghosts in grey, against grey walls in a grey half-world. Louis fought against the sedatives, fought to clarify his own thoughts, to find his self-control.

The arm guided him out of the doctor's office and this time into the sunlight of a secluded patio. He looked up into the face of Father Charles McWilliams, his old friend from his seminary days. He reached out and touched his cassock.

". . . And one among them shall betray me. Was it you, Charles?" Riel whispered incoherently.

Louis' comment had stung him and McWilliams' face revealed his pain.

"Louis, you'll be all right."

Louis nodded, truly sorry. He knew that Father McWilliams was his friend. "Where is Gabriel?"

"In Montreal. The Bishop feels he should go back to the West, but he refuses."

Louis held McWilliams' arm. "The Bishop, I must talk with the Bishop. Surely I can make *him* understand."

McWilliams grasped Louis' shoulders and looked into the dark brooding eyes of his friend. "Believe me, Louis, we love you, but you need rest. You've been through so much."

Louis leaned over and whispered in McWilliams' ear. "They drug me here, constantly. I can't, I will never get well here. I'm not sure I'm even sick."

Quietly, McWilliams answered. "I will tell the Bishop. Please, Louis, rest. I promise you I'll help. Please be patient."

"I can't stand the drugs. I don't know, I can't remember. You must help me. *Please* help me."

Father McWilliams turned and left the patio, more confused than he could ever remember. Louis did not seem insane. He was being drugged, that was all. He resolved to see the Bishop, but after that he did not know what he would do. He knew he had to do something—Louis loved God and he had a brilliant mind. He could not just leave him and abandon him to this place of madness.

Bishop Bourget was standing when McWilliams entered. His long, crimson robes fell majestically about him. His crucifix caught the sunlight and appeared like a blinding light over his heart.

"I would like to speak with you about Louis," McWilliams said urgently.

"I cannot deal with it right now, Father." The Bishop's voice was impatient, and McWilliams already felt defeated, but he pursued the matter anyway. "Some word, Your Grace. I know what a comfort it would be to him."

The Bishop unfolded his hands and turned to the papers on his desk, shuffling them nervously. "Tell him that God will not abandon him. His mission is marked out for him . . . but he *must* be patient."

McWilliams persisted. "Your Grace, please . . . could you put it in a note? It would mean so much . . ."

The Bishop looked up into the young cleric's eyes. He was exasperated with this whole affair . . . what difficulty this whole business had caused. "I will do as you ask, Father, but understand me clearly and make no mistake. I suffer for Louis' mental anguish. But I am *not* unhappy that at this particular time, the church is spared his politics. If the country is to be torn apart over the issue of the West, I prefer that the blame be laid where it belongs—not on a French Catholic, but on an English Protestant. Now, what shall I write? Let's make it quick—our beloved Prime Minister is soon to honour me with a visit."

"Dear Louis," the Bishop wrote, "You are in good hands. It is the best place for you now. God will not abandon you in the hour of your need. Pray and be patient, and the Lord will bring to you a sign. In time, your purpose will be revealed, be patient."

Bishop Bourget replaced the quill in its holder and handed the letter to McWilliams. "May this help our Louis," he said. "And please, speak to that Dumont person and see if you can persuade him to go home. He must be made to believe that we can and will take care of his friend."

In a swirl of crimson the Bishop turned and walked from his office into his private garden. The Prime Minister was just being shown through the gates opposite.

"Thank you for coming, Sir John." The Bishop took the Prime Minister's hand.

"Thank *you*, Bishop Bourget. The country seems calm enough at the moment. A trip to Montreal is always most pleasant."

"I am counting on that calm, Sir John," he said, looking into the Prime Minister's eyes. "There is the matter of separate schools—for those who prefer them, of course—in our new province of Manitoba."

The Prime Minister was careful, the right choice of words was always necessary with the Bishop. "That would be up to the governor, Bishop Bourget. Education, as you know, is a provincial matter."

The Bishop studied Sir John's face. "A government representative put forward by you might be influential when the governor considers the question."

Sir John was interested. He rubbed his chin. "It's something to think about."

The Bishop continued slowly, "There is a Métis named Charles Nolin, who would be eminently qualified . . . I believe quite acceptable."

"I see," said Sir John, careful not to commit himself.

"It would be a great comfort to all French Catholics to know that in the West there is some representation by their . . ." He paused. ". . . own kind."

The Prime Minister nodded. "I'm sure, Bishop." A little trade thought the Prime Minister. A tame Métis to replace the brilliant Louis Riel for the support of the church in Quebec. He would have to make inquiries.

They moved to a lovely rose bush. The Bishop reached out to it and turned to the Prime Minister. Again he spoke slowly, clearly. "This vine was a favourite of mine. I planted it myself. But it grew large and unruly and threatened all the other flowers. It distressed me, and I had to cut it back. Now my garden is under control, but a little sunshine could help the smaller flowers somewhat, don't you think?"

What a metaphor, Macdonald thought. The Bishop was a good politician indeed.

"You may be right, Bishop. A little sunshine can work wonders."

Bourget half smiled. "Nolin, Charles Nolin. Tea, Sir John?"

Father McWilliams moved along the path toward the Third Station of the Cross. Here, on the grounds of the seminary, the Stations of the Cross were arranged along a wooded path, interspersed with clumps of flowers and giant rocks. It was the ideal place to meditate. Even in the winter when it was damp, cold, and lonely and the trees were bare, McWilliams found solace there. On this late summer evening he chose to do his devotions outside, under God's roof. He paused momentarily to watch a black squirrel scurry up a nearby tree. The freedom of all things under heaven weighed on his mind.

He looked up and was startled to see Gabriel Dumont standing in front of him.

"When did you last see Louis?" Dumont asked in a harsh tone.

"Gabriel! I thought you'd gone." He was surprised and a little relieved to see him. Dumont always gave off an aura of strength, of calm and reason. Above all, he was a practical man, like himself.

"Louis has not gone. I have not gone," Gabriel said matter-of-factly.

"I saw him some days ago," McWilliams answered. He felt guilty for not having gone again after he delivered the Bishop's letter.

"I saw him this morning," Dumont said. "They are killing him there, he needs rest, not what they give him."

McWilliams nodded. "He is not well, Gabriel, he is not well."

Dumont looked neither angry nor distressed. "Some Indians," he said patiently, "smoke a certain plant from their pipes. It makes the head cloudy and the body numb.

131

Then they talk wild, they scream and they dance. Later they sleep, and when they wake up they can't remember."

McWilliams listened with interest to Dumont. "They wouldn't give him anything harmful," he protested, wanting to believe it himself.

"They didn't want me to see him," Dumont said. "Finally they say yes, if I promise to go away and not come back."

"It is dangerous for you too, Gabriel. Some people would like to find you."

Dumont was not to be distracted with warnings about his own pursuers. "Louis was in a stupor, crying like a baby, trying to refuse the medicine. He ripped this off his neck." Dumont held out a crucifix. " 'Give this to McWilliams' he said. So here, what does it mean to you?"

McWilliams reached for the crucifix and held it for a moment. "I gave it to Louis when he left the seminary."

Gabriel measured the man before him. "If it has meaning to you, you must help. You must come with me now to the asylum."

McWilliams nodded. He knew Dumont was right. Oh God, he must be right.

"Yes, but we will need money. Wait here for me. I will return in a short time and then we will go."

Dr. Roy looked into McWilliams' face. He did not like this sudden change of plans. Still, McWilliams was the Bishop's assistant.

"His intentions are good . . ." Dr. Roy spoke of Louis in his clinical tone ". . . but there is a delusional pattern in his behaviour which, under certain circumstances, could recur. I simply can't be responsible if you remove him from our care."

McWilliams adjusted his cassock and, feigning impatience, continued, "There is a position for him in the United States . . . a settlement in Montana. They need a teacher, and Louis is qualified."

132

Dr. Roy paused, his annoyance obvious. "It is highly unusual to . . ."

McWilliams interrupted. "The church committed him and the church will be responsible. Would you prefer the Bishop to cut short more pressing matters to come here himself and arrange this?" He hoped his bluff would work. In his calling he had little opportunity to become an accomplished liar.

Dr. Roy reluctantly pulled a cord near his desk and an attendant stood at the door. "Have Mr. Louis David prepared to leave." His voice was full of authority. McWilliams breathed more easily. It had worked. Louis would soon be free.

The half-hour passed slowly. McWilliams glanced out the window several times. Down beyond the gate he could see the carriage and his anticipation grew with his impatience.

Finally Louis entered with the attendant. He was dressed neatly in a dark brown suit with his customary high white collar. The moccasins were gone and he was wearing shoes. He still looked dazed, like a man taken from a heavy sleep. He stumbled forward and embraced McWilliams. The attendant handed him a bundle, a pitifully small bundle considering it contained a man's worldly possessions. "Come," McWilliams said softly. "Come."

Together they walked down the great stone steps of the asylum and into the morning sun. Louis squinted. It seemed so terribly terribly bright after weeks in a world of shadows. Even in the morning sun his pupils remained dilated. "Gabriel!" he said weakly to the driver of the carriage. "Oh Gabriel, I knew you would save me." Louis sank into the seat and McWilliams waved to the driver.

He prayed he had done the right thing. He prayed Dumont would look after Louis, would keep him away from his enemies and away from Canada.

All the way back to Montreal McWilliams thought of

Louis. The man's face, his eyes haunted him. Was he really mad? Why would a madman fight so against such mind-dulling drugs? How could a madman speak with such logic? Visions, McWilliams thought, visions. If visions made a man mad, then all the saints of God's holy church must have been mad too. No. The world was mad, Louis was sane.

The Bishop paced his office, his crimson robes flying with every turn. "Stupid, stupid, stupid!" He spoke to the wall, which did not grace him with an answer. The door opened and McWilliams entered.

"You summoned me, Your Grace?"

The Bishop turned on him. "You had Riel released?" Was he really such a fool?

McWilliams looked down, deeply surprised. The plush red carpet stared back accusingly at him. He raised his head and met the Bishop's eyes.

"I thought Your Grace would be pleased."

The Bishop raised his hand to his forehead. The fool, the fool. "It was . . . critical . . . to his condition that he be kept in custody. Those were my orders!"

"Quite right, Your Grace. But then, his condition changed. His sanity returned."

"Returned?" the Bishop seethed. McWilliams could not remember ever having heard the Bishop like this before.

"Miraculously," he replied calmly. "And his sense of purpose as well. It can only be attributed to your kind letter."

"My letter?" The Bishop paled and bit his lower lip. "And where is my letter now?"

McWilliams smiled. "I imagine he carries it with him as a memento, Your Grace." The Bishop was trapped.

"Where has he gone?" His tone was a little more conciliatory now.

"I'm not really sure . . ." McWilliams thought for a second and decided that another lie would be necessary.

"He said he would travel for a while, Your Grace. First to the eastern United States, then perhaps to Europe for a time, then to the western United States. I think he has been offered a teaching position."

The Bishop was perplexed. "He will not try to return to Canada?"

"No, Your Grace." McWilliams felt the full joy of a certain success. "I told you, his sanity has returned. A sane man in Louis' position would not return to imminent danger. In time, people will forget, perhaps there will be an amnesty."

The Bishop measured his young assistant carefully. Perhaps, he wondered, perhaps he had taught this young man too well.

13

Escape to the South

Though it rain gold and silver in a foreign land and daggers and spears at home, yet it is better to be at home.

A Malay proverb

The wagon edged south over the dirt road and passed uneventfully from Quebec into Maine. Here the road followed the Kennebec River, winding around placid lakes and passing through small villages. The first frost had come and virgin forests of maple and sumach trees blazed with autumn colours. Some still green, others gold, yellow, orange, and bright red, the trees of Maine glowed in their short-lived glory.

In Maine, Riel and Dumont stayed with a Father Bouchet for a few days. He was a Métis priest whose family had long ago settled in New England. Here, through a series of friends, they had arranged their onward journey.

"It is better to travel a circuitous route," Father Bouchet advised. "You will find few enemies here, but Montana may be too close to home yet. You have some money, take your time."

"I have a mission," Louis persisted. "I must return to the West."

"You're not going back to Canada," Gabriel said firmly. "Not until there is an amnesty in writing, not until Tom Scott is forgotten."

Louis despaired. "What of my mission, my plan for the oppressed of the world?"

"It'll wait until you are not among them," was Gabriel's reply.

"It's true," Louis said half-heartedly, "Bishop Bourget said I would receive a sign."

Gabriel made no comment. To disagree with the Bishop of Montreal would not help calm Louis down. To agree with him would be to accept his double-dealings.

"First you should go to Massachusetts," Father Bouchet suggested. "There is a small French community in Worcester, and I have arranged for you to stay with Father Primeau, the church rector."

Louis looked lonely and forlorn. The fact that he had been officially exiled from the land of his birth, from his people, and from what he considered his destiny had not yet sunk in. His eyes still bore the haunted, vacant look of his recent terrible experiences.

"Then," Father Bouchet continued, "you will go to Washington. There you will stay with Pierre Mallet and his family."

"How long?" Louis inquired. "When can I go home?"

"You will be several months in Washington. Then your passage by train will be arranged and you can go onward to Montana."

Louis was totally dejected, deep in his own depression. Gabriel watched him carefully. They had not been gone long and Louis was still exhausted.

"Pierre will tell you about Montana. It's all being arranged."

Father Bouchet spoke to Louis with great kindness, as though he were a child to be led through the wilderness. For the first time since leaving Montreal, Gabriel felt calmer. Louis would be safe now and he would get well.

As each day passed, Gabriel's hope grew. Louis slept more and ate more and talked of his mission less. Normalcy began to return to his eyes, the colour to his skin.

"Tell me about Moses, Uncle Louis!" Pierre Mallet's little daughter was a wonder to behold. Her eyes shone like large chestnuts and her hair was long, thick, and well combed. She was eight years old, this "Washington Métis," whose father was an Indian agent. She went from Louis to Gabriel, one told her bible stories, the other, tales of the buffalo hunt, and she loved them all.

Louis was patient with her and they often talked or played for hours on end.

"The child brings back his health," Gabriel said to Mallet. "She is the medicine he needs."

Mallet smiled and agreed heartily. "Children do not judge, they receive openly and love without prerequisite those who love them."

Dumont now relaxed even more.

"I have arranged passage," Mallet said. "And a job as well." Gabriel smiled, "You have been good to us, Mallet, very good."

"The job is as a teacher in a small Indian school near Helena, in Montana. It doesn't pay too much, but I have also arranged to have Louis live with a Métis family."

Dumont sipped the red wine slowly. "When it is finished, I will leave him and go back to the buffalo."

Mallet nodded. "It is good. He must begin to build his own life again. He has had too many disappointments."

Gabriel agreed. "It is strange, but Louis did everything right. He established the territorial government by their law, he tried Scott by their law, he was elected to Parliament by their law—and he never hurt anyone. He just prayed all the time."

"It is terrible to do things right and have them turn out so badly."

Gabriel agreed. "It nearly destroyed him. He will never understand why the *anglais* wouldn't listen. You can take a coyote and raise him from a pup, feed him and care for him, but it doesn't matter, he's still a wild animal. He might turn on you, he might not. If he doesn't, it's because he is well fed, not because you have destroyed his instinct."

Mallet agreed. "The English have one instinct—to take Indian and Métis land."

"Is it different with the Americans?" Gabriel asked.

"Not for the Indian, but for the Métis," Mallet began. "The Americans think all Indians are stupid. They don't see the Métis as Indian though. We are French to them."

Gabriel nodded. "Some animals eat meat, others eat grass," and they laughed together.

In a few days they left Washington by train and headed west. Louis sat by the window and stared out. He did not begin to smile until the train hit the flatlands of the great American prairies, and then he began to feel at home again.

They left the train in Cheyenne, Wyoming, and from there travelled on horseback across Wyoming and up into Montana. Gabriel too felt the freedom of the life he knew; it was good to have a saddle beneath him again and the great sky above.

Louis had never been a good horseman, but on this trip he improved and even seemed to enjoy himself. Some nights they spent with the Sioux, for Dumont spoke their language and understood their ways. Those were good nights, because they slept under the stars or in a teepee, and there was always dancing and singing and stories—stories of the plains before the white man, before his cavalry and his guns and his diseases.

Other nights they spent in frontier towns, which were dusty and struggling for their survival. When they drank in the saloon the cowboys called Dumont "Frenchie," and he laughed with them.

Finally, after weeks of travel, they arrived at the home of Jean Monette, where Louis was to remain. The man was good-natured and kind, as was his very understanding wife. They were open as only the Métis were open with their brothers, and Gabriel sensed he had brought Louis to a place where he could live in peace.

For his part, Louis seemed reconciled to his exile. This, Gabriel supposed, had something to do with Marguerite, Monette's lovely daughter.

"She is a good-looking woman," Gabriel said to Louis. "You need a wife, someone to make a home for you, eh?"

Louis actually blushed. "Do you think God wills it?" he asked.

"Why else would He have brought you together?" Gabriel replied. He thought of his own wife, Madeleine, for he had been away over half a year.

"Well, Louis, you have your school now and your young students. I think soon you may have a wife, too. This is where we part, my friend, you to your teaching, I to my hunting." Gabriel felt the tears welling up in his eyes.

Louis held out his hands. "Be patient, Gabriel, and love our people. As you once told me, we will be together again." They shook hands simply and parted.

"He will always be your friend," Marguerite offered.

Louis watched the figure disappearing in the distance. "God will send me a sign," he said, "God will send me a sign."

14

The Second Coming, 1884

*Faith in the supernatural is a desperate wager
made by man at the lowest ebb of his fortunes.*
George Santayana

Jean Tremblay turned the meat slowly, and as he did
so, bits of fat caused the fire to crackle.

"We could have got there tonight," Napoleon Nault
said.

Gabriel Dumont leaned against his saddle and chewed
on a piece of meat. "No need. Things won't be any
worse tomorrow than they are today."

"Better to let him think a while," said Pierre. "Maybe
he won't want to come with us, got a wife now, and
kids too."

"I hope the years have been good to Louis," said
Gabriel.

Napoleon smiled. "He'll come, we all belong together.
Been apart too long."

"Fifteen years is a long time, but the exile's over."
Pierre was too young to remember Louis Riel, but he'd
heard stories over and over.

Dumont shrugged. "He's American now, maybe he
should stay. We'll ask him, that's all, just ask."

Henri took the meat that Tremblay offered him and
leaned back against the still warm rock. "He must come,
he must. We need him to speak for us now, things are
getting worse every day."

Gabriel shook his head. "Smart of us to think we could start again, eh? That land, hell, even the buffalo weren't dumb enough to stick around. It's that Charles Nolin." Dumont's voice grew low and angry. "He's a bad one; we knew it in Red River years ago. *Chien!* Supposed to be our government 'representative.' He should take care of us the way he look after himself."

"No food, no timber contracts, but they got enough money to send the Mounted Police to see we obey the law . . ." Pierre was sitting up and speaking to the fire.

"Crozier, that Policeman fellow, he's not so bad." Gabriel Dumont had a certain respect for Major Crozier. They had done some hunting together and Gabriel had sometimes translated Cree for him.

"He's not so bad . . ." Pierre said, "It's what he stands for." Dumont did not disagree. That, after all, was why they had written to Louis and why they were going to see him now.

"We're not so far now, how come we wait until tomorrow?" Napoleon was anxious to see his old hero. He had grown into manhood loving Riel, and for him he was bigger than life.

"'Cause we come too late, better in the morning." Dumont had been purposely riding slowly all day. In the end he decided he wanted another night under the stars to think. He prayed that Riel was doing well and that he was healthy. The Métis needed Louis, they had lost their spark, they were a beaten people. They needed something, someone . . . a torch they still remembered and talked about. He himself could lead them in most ways, but he couldn't read or speak with them like Louis. The heart, thought Gabriel, was missing the head.

As the five riders came over the hill they saw the small schoolhouse nestled in the valley. A lone figure stood in the doorway, and Gabriel knew it was Louis.

The two men embraced and then Napoleon and Jean Tremblay embraced their hero and long-time friend.

The others were introduced and Louis politely shook each of their hands. Gabriel was pleased. Louis' hair was still thick and dark, his skin had good colour. He even looked a bit fuller in the face and body.

"She's put some meat on your bones!" Gabriel laughed mockingly, pinching Louis' arm.

"She is, as you said, Gabriel, a good woman."

Dumont moved away from the others, guiding Louis by the arm. "Let's walk a little and talk, it's been a long time." The two men moved off.

"What does Marguerite think?" Gabriel asked.

"Marguerite is Métis. She understands what our people need. Living here she knows the importance of a piece of land, the recognition of who you are and the freedom to live the way you want."

"Then she agrees to your coming back?"

"Of course. We both knew it was only a matter of time . . . of God deciding when it should take place."

Dumont knew Louis would not refuse their request, but still, he had expected more surprise. He should have known better, he thought. At heart Louis was still the dreamer. He looked deeply into Louis' calm eyes. "We'd be starting all over again, Louis."

Louis appeared confident. "Not quite. This time there is a plan . . . for me, for our people, for all the oppressed people of the world. This time, my old friend, we do it right, we do it right from the beginning."

Louis' voice had the strength of former days. Dumont felt drawn to his words.

"So," he said, "it is definite, you'll come back with us."

Louis paused and his tone suggested he was speaking of someone else, something else. "God wants you to know you have chosen the right way. Now there are five of you, and you arrived on the fifth day of the month. You wish to have a sixth return with you . . . so you must wait until the sixth . . . tomorrow morning . . . then I'll give you my decision."

Gabriel was a bit puzzled, but decided that Louis had become even more superstitious than before. Great minds, he thought, think in strange ways.

In the morning Louis formally agreed to return to his people and they loaded everything into the wagons and left for the Saskatchewan country.

As they approached the village of Batoche, Louis leaned forward in the wagon. A huge crowd had assembled with their carts, perhaps five or six hundred Métis in all. The adults cheered wildly and yelled, "Long live Riel! Long live the Métis nation! Long live Gabriel Dumont!" As he came near, part of the huge crowd rushed over to touch him and pat him on the back. Louis was overcome, tears ran from his eyes and he bent over to reach out to his many old friends, and to others who knew him only in story or in song. The children all stared at him curiously, but clapped their hands wildly, imitating their joyous elders. Louis had never realized in his wildest dreams that coming home to his people would be so sweet.

It was the New Jerusalem, a people waiting for their messiah and spiritual leader to return.

Old Ouellette then greeted Louis, his wrinkled face grinning broadly. "I am ninety-four today, Louis," the old man said proudly, "I been staying around to fight with Louis Riel." Louis smiled, and Gabriel patted Ouellette on the shoulder. "We got to get rid of him soon. This old man's expensive—been through thirty horses and five women and done 'um all in!" Everyone laughed with Ouellette, the oldest man in Batoche and a legend in his own right.

"And what first, Louis?" Gabriel asked.

"Pens and paper, Gabriel, pens and paper."

"You get your pens and papers, I get the men, right?"

Louis gave Gabriel a long and searching look. "For now, twelve men, twelve will do for now."

Gabriel rode off, thinking that Louis had a flare for

the dramatic, not to mention his new penchant for numbers. Twelve, thirteen, one hundred! What did it matter?

Louis kneeled at the altar. Father Ritchot, who had followed his people west to Batoche, watched Louis pray.

Poor Louis, Father Ritchot thought. Perhaps he will do better this time. Father Ritchot did not know what to think or what to do. The Bishop had told him not to let Louis come back, but Louis was here. The people had gone for him, and what was he to do?

Slowly Louis rose from the altar. He had tears in his eyes as he turned to Father Ritchot. "I have come to do God's work," he said to the old priest.

"Are you sure?" Father Ritchot asked. He did not know what else to say; Louis had always been so devout, maybe God did speak to him. Who was he to answer such a question.

"I am sure, Father," Louis replied. "Bishop Bourget told me to wait for a sign . . . and the sign has been given." Father Ritchot made the sign of the cross and Louis departed.

Dumont was waiting outside with the horses as he had been told to do. "Now where?" he inquired, as Louis mounted.

"First to the telegraph office and then to Assywin."

Dumont looked at Louis for only a second. "The Dreamer?"

"Yes, the Dreamer," Louis replied.

The evening was cold and the snow on the ground crunched under the horses' feet as the men approached the Indian camp. A fog had settled in near the water and it rose from the ground, giving the surroundings a surreal quality. In the Indian village the smoke curled above the teepees and blended with the fog.

"Wait here," Louis told Dumont and the men. "I must see Assywin alone."

"Are you sure?" Dumont asked.

"Wait here," he answered.

Gabriel turned his horse up toward the trees on the left. The others stayed where they were in sight of the Indian village, watching as Louis rode off into the distance.

"What the hell's he up to, Gabriel?" The voice surprised Dumont, and he found himself looking into the face of Major L. N. F. Crozier, the head of the Mounted Police detachment.

"I better learn to watch out for you," said Gabriel. "You getting quiet like a Cree."

Crozier looked at Dumont. "Louis Riel," he said sternly. "He's got quite a reputation."

"The kind he's got with your people he doesn't deserve."

Crozier nodded. "It's none of my business now, Gabriel, as long as he obeys the law."

"Louis knows the law," Dumont answered.

"I don't know if I like him talking too much with old Assywin though." Crozier was guarded.

Dumont was guarded too. "They're just old friends. He's come to pay his respects."

Crozier mounted his horse. "Tell him to keep it social," he said. Dumont nodded. He wondered himself why Louis wanted to see the Dreamer. They weren't really such old friends.

Inside the teepee, Louis sat with Assywin. He looked as he had before into the scarred face of the man who had once frightened him so terribly. The Dreamer's eyes were closed. He sat with his legs crossed and chanted slowly as he rocked back and forth.

Louis was speaking in a low voice, almost in tune with Assywin.

"It is not too late . . . your dead warriors and ours . . . we will rise up in a glorious army in Christ! The Cree and the Blackfoot are our brothers. Your mothers were our mothers. Join us and together we will be strong."

Assywin opened his eyes slowly and looked at Louis. In the distance a coyote howled. "You have come on the night of the ghosts," he said, motioning outside. "It is good. It is right." He handed Louis the knife, then appeared to go into a deep trance. Louis took the knife and cut his arm. The blood spurted and ran quickly down to his wrist. Assywin took the knife and slit his own arm and clasped arms with Louis.

The blood was mixed; it was done.

15

A Taste of Victory

Peoples and governments have never learned anything from history, or acted on principles deduced from it.

Hegel

Donald Smith and Sir John A. Macdonald stood in the railway yard. The morning was cold, but the sky was a deep blue and the sun reflected off the great hulk of steel parked on the siding. When the two men exhaled, their breath emerged like smoke from a pipe and disappeared into the clear frosty air.

"What a magnificent machine!" Sir John rubbed his hand along the cold steel of the great engine. "And lying dormant, hidden deep within its heart, is the very future of this country. We can't stop now, Donald, we can't stop!"

Smith looked at the engine—it was his dream too, but somehow he didn't quite view it in the same way as Sir John. "Sir John, the Privy Council was our last hope. The creditors, they demand payment, otherwise they'll seize the stock and . . ." He paused and looked sadly at the engine before he continued, "the equipment."

"They must not!" Sir John's voice rose. "Damn the Opposition! Damn those stupid, short-sighted sonsof-bitches!"

Smith nodded. The dream of the great transcontinental railway, the dream they had both held for years, was

148

bogged down in a hopeless struggle for funds. "It's frustrating," he said, "terribly, terribly frustrating."

"Frustrating? It's stupid! How can this nation grow up? We have to be united, we have to be united by a transportation system that will serve the needs of the whole country and make it possible to settle the West."

"I know, Sir John, I know," Smith said softly.

"I'm sorry," the Prime Minister said, "I know you've given this thing your all. It's hardly your fault. I just can't make those dottering fools understand what they're sitting on. My God man, the potential this country has is staggering! If only *this* country and *those* politicians could get bloody well together!"

- Smith put his gloved hands into his pockets and looked at Sir John. "Sir, what are we going to do about the creditors?"

"I really don't know, Donald, I just don't know."

The two men turned and headed back toward the Hill. The Houses of Parliament looked elegant in the morning sunlight as they crossed Wellington Street.

"Amazing," Sir John mumbled, "simply amazing."

"What?" asked Smith, paying little attention.

"It's amazing that a place with so much dignity could be filled with so many idiots!"

Smith smiled. He always enjoyed it when Sir John was riding the Opposition. As they entered the Prime Minister's office and discarded their heavy fur-trimmed coats, Sir John turned to him.

"Apart from the creditors taking away our railroad, what other happy news do you have for me this fine morning?"

Smith had forgotten the dispatch in his jacket, and as he thought about it, he smiled.

"I have a dispatch here. Just a minute." He withdrew it from his coat and unfolded it. "It's another petition from the West demanding redress for grievances."

"More semi-literate demands for land settlements, I suppose." The Prime Minister was so occupied with the railway he was bored with everything else, and definitely bored with land grievances from the Indians and Métis.

"No," Smith said, "this one's really very well written . . . and it's signed by Louis Riel. Remember him?"

The Prime Minister shook his head in exasperation. "Good God! That's all I need! Riel back again?"

Smith folded the paper. "I'll just send it on to the Ministry."

The Prime Minister suddenly looked brighter. His eyes shone with a glint Smith had not seen for some months.

"No, wait. Let me see that. Let me see Riel's petition."

"Just idle threats, Sir John, nothing to be taken seriously."

Sir John muttered as he read: "Control of natural resources, changes to the homestead laws, amnesty for 1870, compensation for malicious treatment of the Métis by Wolseley's troops in 1870, guaranteed land rights for the Métis, and . . . Good God! He's suggesting separation, Donald!"

But Smith felt there were more urgent problems. "Sir John, the creditors! Could we decide what they're going to be told?"

The Prime Minister looked his friend in the eye and a smile crept across his face. "Parliament, Donald, Parliament. Remember how Riel angered them before? Can you imagine how they'd react if his new threats grow into a dangerous situation?"

Smith looked at Sir John with amazement. "You wouldn't?"

Sir John simply smiled his half-smile. "I certainly would. Those dolts must come to realize that the railway is vital to national security. Besides, it won't take much doing. A suggestion here, a well-designed scenario there. If they understand what could happen, perhaps they'll see to it we finish the railway so it won't happen."

"I doubt Riel and his group are really a threat to the security of this nation, Sir John." Smith was not

150

entirely comfortable with Sir John's plan, for it would imply outright rejection of the Métis and Indian demands, and at this critical moment, rejection could be dangerous for the future of the Northwest.

"I think this 'situation' will build a little fire under Parliament," said Sir John slyly.

"Let us hope it does not start a major one on the prairies, Sir John—one we cannot control."

Dumont sat before the small fire and watched the coffee heating up. He had been out gathering men, alerting them to possible trouble ahead. They had all responded to his reasoning and to the name of their hero, Louis Riel. The Métis were gathering at Batoche. Louis called it "a demonstration of determination."

It was still bitterly cold, but dressed in his warm buffalo hides and camped in the shelter of the rocks before the fire, Gabriel was warm. Even so, he wished he was back in his own home with Madeleine. He saw Major Crozier's horse approaching in the full light of the moon. Crozier dismounted, but Dumont did not rise.

"Seems you always know where to find me these days."

"When I can't find you, that's when I'll worry," Crozier replied with a smile.

"Coffee?" Gabriel extended a hot tin cup of the steaming brew.

"Thanks." The Major sat down cross-legged next to Gabriel.

"It's been quiet up to now, Gabriel. Not the way you and I might like it, but at least quiet.

Gabriel looked into Crozier's face. "Major, you're a fair man. I know you a long time now. You know the Métis can't be still forever. We got no land rights, we got no work, there are no buffalo left. We deserve better."

The Major nodded. He was no admirer of the politicians in Ottawa, or their priorities.

151

"They make a lot of promises," Gabriel said flatly. "They don't keep their promises."

Crozier knew that only too well. Time and time again he had found himself enforcing broken promises.

"In time," Crozier began, "in time it will be different."

Dumont looked at the man squarely. "You don't believe that, Major."

"Maybe not, Gabriel, maybe not. But I have a job to do and you could help me. I'd rather have it that way."

"I don't say yes, I don't say no. What's on your mind, Major?"

Crozier began, and he chose his words carefully. "Some of your people have loose tongues and big imaginations. They've got my men a little jumpy."

"*Some* people had it pretty good before Louis came. Some people would like to see him go." Gabriel deliberately emphasized the word "some." He waited for Crozier to make his next move.

"They're gonna get their way," Crozier said. "I have an order signed by the Prime Minister that says unless Riel's gone, I have to arrest him."

Dumont was not really surprised. Louis' name must stick like a craw in that old hoot's throat. "On what grounds?" he asked Crozier. Dumont was now on a fishing trip for information.

"What does it matter?" Crozier replied.

"On what grounds?" Gabriel demanded again.

Crozier thought for a moment, trying to decide if there was any good reason why Dumont should not be told. Maybe he cared enough about Riel to get him out of the country, and that, he figured, could save one hell of a lot of trouble.

"They say he's a threat to the security of the country."

Dumont looked into Crozier's eyes once again, and this time it was a cold, hard look. "Maybe this country needs a threat. Maybe the Métis need to be a threat. Louis calls it 'a demonstration of determination.' Well,

Major Crozier, you better get a warrant for about one thousand Métis and maybe a couple thousand Indians. We're just as 'determined' as Louis.''

I should have known better, Crozier thought to himself. Dumont was no man to play follow the leader to some religious fanatic. Dumont was a leader, a strong, independent man. There would be no chance to influence him.

"Look, Dumont, you know me. You know how I feel. I'm telling you all this because whatever's behind it I don't intend to question my orders.''

"*I* question your orders," he said, matter-of-factly, "but I don't expect *you* to.''

Crozier smiled at Dumont. "You have more freedom than I. I must obey my orders. If he isn't gone by tomorrow, I must come and get him.''

Good luck, Gabriel thought, good luck. He knew full well there were only forty-six men in the whole detachment, and that reinforcements from Regina were not yet on their way. What he didn't know was that Louis had already heard from Ottawa, and that he had passed the message, with all its insulting rejections, on to the Dreamer.

Gabriel decided to be back in Batoche in the morning. Plenty of time to organize things, plenty of time to plan Louis' "demonstration of determination.''

Miles away across the prairie, another fire burned, this one a giant, with flames leaping toward the distant sky. Old Assywin stood before it, arms extended, eyes open, and head tilted upward toward the great bear star. He sang the song that warriors of his people had sung for generations. He raised his praises to dead ancestors who twinkled in the sky above. Drums beat steadily and the rattle of the medicine man's baton cracked and hissed like a rattlesnake. Chalk-white faces danced and raised their ceremonial tomahawks . . . a pile of rifles lay within easy reach.

At midnight, when the moon was high and full, the now-silent warriors poured forth from the village. Old Assywin looked after his son, Wandering Spirit, as he disappeared into the darkness.

Many miles across the prairie from Batoche, the sun came up on the isolated settlement of Frog Lake. It was Sunday morning and Father Marchand was saying mass. He turned from the altar and raised the chalice toward the congregation. He was startled to see Wandering Spirit, *L'esprit errant*, sitting in the front pew in battle paint and full war regalia. Half-a-dozen other warriors stood in various places around the small church. The members of the congregation, many of them Cree and Ojibwa, sat nervously attempting to say their prayers while Wandering Spirit, the tails of his war bonnet touching the front of the pew, sat and stared directly ahead.

When the mass was finished, Father Marchand stepped forward. He spoke in Cree. "We are glad to have the great warrior Wandering Spirit worship among us. We hope he and his braves come in peace . . ." He had intended to continue, but Wandering Spirit rose, and facing the white half of the congregation, shouted "*Neá*! Go! Leave this place of your God!" Then he strode down the aisle, motioning his braves to follow.

The congregation did as they were told. "Who does that savage think he is?" one of them murmured. "Where are the Police?" another asked.

When they got outside, Wandering Spirit turned to them. "Which of you is the agent, Thomas Quinn?" Quinn, a soft-spoken man who had run the Hudson's Bay post for three years, stepped forward. "I am Quinn."

"Get your keys and open the post!" Wandering Spirit shouted.

"No," Quinn replied, knowing that fear was no way to deal with the Indians.

Wandering Spirit's eyes narrowed. "Get the keys, we take the guns."

Quinn could feel the keys in his pocket, but he lied. "I don't have them and I won't get them." Mrs. Quinn screamed out from the crowd, "Give him the keys, Tom!" Her scream coincided with the shot from Wandering Spirit's rifle. Quinn, shot from point-blank range, fell down face deep in the snow.

"Stop! No! Stop!" Father Marchand raced across the snow from the front of the church. Wandering Spirit stopped him with a single shot, and he crumpled, a heap of black on a field of white snow.

The whites broke from their ranks and ran for their houses.

A few made it, but most did not.

Big Bear, the chief of the Crees, reached out and grabbed his brother's arm. "Don't kill any more," he pleaded. "There is no need . . ." Wandering Spirit's eyes were glazed. He neither saw nor heard Big Bear. He saw only Assywin's scarred face, heard only the distant cries of a hundred dying Indian babies, their papooses infected with the white man's diseases. His people were starving, the buffalo were gone, the land was desolate.

Wandering Spirit shook loose and turned to face Big Bear. "Why not kill them?" he asked, without emotion.

By late afternoon the Indians had gone, taking their hostages. Two houses were burned, together with the small church. The survivors of the small community, three in all, looked about them and wept. One of them, William Cameron, beat out a somewhat incoherent message on the telegraph.

At his headquarters in Battleford, Major Crozier read the message and closed his eyes. "My God," he sighed. "It's really happening." He bit his lip hard. What a damn position to be in! He tried to think what could be defended and what could not. Have to get people into Prince Albert, round up some volunteers. He remembered Riel's meeting with Assywin—well, now he had to get Riel. Riel was the match that had lit the flame.

He wondered what good it would do to break the match now.

Gabriel Dumont rode into Batoche. He had smoked the pipe with Poundmaker and talked with Big Bear. The men he had recruited preceded him and were all gathered in Batoche, waiting. As he rode down the snow-covered street he was surprised to see a huge crowd in front of the telegraph office. What the hell was going on?

The answer came all too soon. The Northwest Rebellion had begun.

Moiese Ouellette sat on his horse at the edge of the crowd, his leathery face a mask that betrayed no emotion. He turned his head as Gabriel approached, and a hum of acknowledgement ran through the crowd of mounted horsemen and standing onlookers.

"What's happening, Ouellette?"

"Jean, he intercept a telegram. The Indians attack Frog Lake and kill a bunch of *anglais* and some priests."

Dumont was stunned. It could not have been Poundmaker, the leader of the Cree, they had only just smoked the pipe. Poundmaker had agreed to get guns from certain Hudson's Bay posts, but not yet, and there were to be no massacres.

"Big Bear?" he asked Ouellette.

"He was there," Ouellette answered.

"Wandering Spirit!" Suddenly Gabriel knew what had happened. He realized a pact of mutual protection between Riel and Assywin was a mistake. "Where's Louis?"

"He's in there," Ouellette said, pointing to the telegraph office. "Told us to gather up everybody and he'd come out and talk. Guess he's thinking what to say."

Gabriel dismounted and walked into the telegraph office. Louis was alone, his face pale and worn.

"You always come when I need you," he said simply.

Gabriel smiled. "You gonna need me quite a bit now."

"The Prime Minister turned down our petition," Louis said. "They sent back an insulting reply. I showed it to Assywin."

Gabriel let out a quiet breath. "And Wandering Spirit went to Frog Lake for guns—and revenge."

Louis nodded. "I tried to reason with them. I didn't want this."

"I know," he answered. "You always want to talk."

"Maybe they'll listen now," Louis said. "I've been writing a telegram to the Prime Minister . . ."

"They don't want to listen, Louis." Gabriel's voice had an emphatic tone. "Major Crozier's got an order for your arrest. He'll probably try to travel by night. If he doesn't run into anything on the way, he'll be here tomorrow."

Louis looked blankly at Dumont. "Perhaps if I talked to him . . ." Gabriel interrupted. "There's no more time for talk, my friend. Are you ready to fight?"

Louis looked at him and thought for a moment. "Is it the only way to achieve my plan—a place for all oppressed people?"

"I'm not sure about your plan, Louis, but I know it's the only way left for the Métis."

Louis nodded again. The look of defeat slowly left his face and was replaced by one of determination. "Well then, go to the church," he said. "We'll have Father Ritchot say mass. Then we will arm ourselves and go out to meet Crozier."

"At last," Gabriel shouted, "at last he has seen the light!"

Together they ran to the church and the others followed. Louis went in first to speak to Father Ritchot. The priest was at prayer, a lone figure before the altar.

"Father Ritchot, I must speak with you."

The priest crossed himself, stood up, and came over to Louis. He looked into the glowing dark eyes, and a feeling of terror ran through him.

157

"I know what has happened," he said to Louis.

"We must fight," Louis said. "Will you say mass for us?" The priest summoned his inner strength. He had known Louis since boyhood, and it was he who had first recognized his innate intelligence.

"When you were young, I knew you were not like the other Métis boys." He spoke slowly, wanting Louis to understand. "I wrote to Father Taché and recommended you for schooling. When there was no money to pay, the church paid. You were my first pupil, Louis. It pains me . . . I . . ."

"They are coming to get me. We must fight," Louis interjected. "Give us mass, Father."

"I do not believe in war, Louis. I do not believe it is necessary for our people to kill other men."

"Give us mass." Louis' voice was shrill now. He was no longer asking, he was demanding.

"No," Father Ritchot said firmly. "I will not bless killing, nor those who are going to do it."

Louis seized the white linen altar cloth and yanked it hard. The candlesticks fell to the floor, and Louis seized the great crucifix. Turning his back on Father Ritchot, he marched quickly out of the church.

"Louis! Louis! Don't do this!" Father Ritchot followed him out the door as the Métis all stood around watching in silence.

Charles Nolin stepped out of the crowd and Dumont spit as he passed.

"Crozier won't back down," Nolin said. Louis turned on him angrily. "Neither will I!"

"If I must, I'll use the church to stop you!" Father Ritchot glanced at the faces he knew so well. "Listen to me! You must not do this! The church is against it!"

Gabriel pushed Nolin roughly aside and stood at Louis' side. "All of you! Either we go with Louis in pride into battle, or we crawl back to what we were!"

Riel raised the great crucifix high in the air. "God

rides with us my brothers! God rides with the Métis people!"

A wild cheer rose from the Métis, and Tremblay, who was mounted and at the edge of the crowd, let out a great whoop. His horse rose up on its hind legs and then he galloped down the main street and turned sharply back toward the crowd. Holding his rifle under his arm and riding hard, he shot off the sign from the Hudson's Bay post.

Riel turned to Dumont. "The die is cast," he said gravely. "There is no turning back for any of us."

Gabriel smiled. "There never was, Louis. There never was."

All day families trooped into Prince Albert while Crozier moved his men to Fort Carlton. Too many damn guns to let them fall into Métis or Indian hands. He would leave and travel by night, he thought, stopping at Duck Lake to secure the arms there. He had some volunteers from Prince Albert. Not enough, but some.

He sat at his desk and worked over his plan. He would decide what to do about Riel after he had secured the guns at the Duck Lake post. He needed reinforcements to take Batoche. No, he decided. The damage was done. Forget Riel. Get the guns and get back to Battleford and wait for help.

He looked up into the eyes of a young man standing before him.

"James Howe, sir. Reporting for duty."

He looked the green recruit over. "How'd you get here, soldier?"

"I came from Battleford, sir. Regina before that."

Crozier rubbed his chin. "Too bad there's only one of you," he said. "What do you know about the reinforcements?"

Young Howe looked puzzled. "I heard there were some due in two weeks, sir. They sent me on ahead."

"How kind of them," Crozier said wearily, "how very kind."

"Here are my orders, sir." Crozier looked at the papers dully. Just what he needed in the middle of an Indian uprising with only forty-six trained men.

"Go get some rest, son, we'll be moving out soon." He took the papers and tossed them aside. Those, he thought, can wait.

16

Ottawa: The Response

*War involves in its progress such a train of unforeseen
and unsupposed circumstances that no human wisdom
can calculate the end. It has but one thing certain,
and that is to increase taxes.*

Thomas Paine

The dispatches telling of the Indian and Métis uprising
reached Ottawa in a matter of hours, first the report on
Wandering Spirit, then Crozier's last desperate telegram.

Donald Smith stood in the wings of the House and
listened to the Prime Minister of Canada.

Sir John's speech reverberated through the House. His
ringing oratory bounced off the heavily panelled walls
and almost shook the great red velvet chair of the
Governor-General.

"I think it's one of his best performances," Smith said
to the Prime Minister's elderly secretary, Mr. Merrit.

"Damn!" Merrit replied, "If I weren't nearly seventy,
I'd bloody well go out and enlist myself."

The House rose and Sir John received a standing
ovation. He picked up his papers and swept down the
aisle to meet Smith.

"Congratulations, Sir John. That was thoroughly rous-
ing." There was a bit of mockery in his voice.

Sir John hissed with amusement and pinched Smith's
arm. "We will get our railroad, won't we? Yes indeed,
Donald. Now they know why they need it."

161

"Sir John," he pleaded, trying to regain a serious perspective, "fighting a war to build a railway is probably not the best way to . . ."

The Prime Minister stared balefully at him. "Damn it man, this country is at war. I did not start it, I did not conduct a massacre, I did not give Louis Riel permission to come back to Canada and start a . . . a . . . rebellion! There's no other way. Now we need the railway and now Parliament will vote us the funds! It's just making the best of a bad mess!"

Smith nodded in agreement. "I was hardly blaming you, Sir John." Together they entered the Prime Minister's office. It was as messy as Smith had ever seen it. Large topographical maps covered the usually clean desk and red pins now dotted the large map of Canada that hung on the wall. Smith was holding the latest dispatches.

"Well," Sir John said, "what do they say?"

"They want to know how serious it really is."

Sir John rubbed his chin. "And you told them that in my judgement we must have at least five thousand troops and their equipment in the West as soon as possible?"

Smith looked at the Prime Minister. "I told them that in *your* judgement, yes. Yes, I told them."

"And you don't agree?"

"I think it's tragic, unfortunate, but I don't think it warrants . . ."

The Prime Minister interrupted. "I trust you did not tell them that."

Smith shook his head. "They didn't ask."

The Prime Minister turned to his giant wall map. "The only way to accomplish this is to complete the railway. How long to Batoche?"

Smith looked at the map carefully. "There are still great gaps, and the railway only goes as far as Qu'Appelle. If we laid track in teams, brought in additional coolies, and walked some of the way, I think it could be done in six weeks."

162

"We can finish it in six weeks? Good. We can have our troops in the West in six weeks *by rail*."

"It is still winter, Sir John."

The Prime Minister smiled. Well, it will be spring when they get there, won't it?"

"It's quite muddy, sir," Smith said flatly. "And we have only open boxcars—it's going to be terribly cold at night."

"May I remind you that we once walked an army to Manitoba."

Smith returned the Prime Minister's look. "May I remind you, it was warmer."

"Yes, yes. You may remind me of anything you want. Just get on with my railroad."

"Sir John, who's going to command the troops?"

The Prime Minister grinned. "General Frederick Middleton, I believe. He's got quite a reputation, a regular soldier and a very good general."

"But he's a 'proper' general, Sir John."

The Prime Minister shook his head. "You and your West, Donald, you make such a mystery out of it. And just what are the disadvantages of a 'proper' general?"

"He's going to use British military strategy, and it just won't work against the Métis. They just don't play by our rules you know."

"Don't worry, Donald. He's just returned from fighting in India. I'm sure he knows how to fight without any rules."

Smith shook his head. "I hope so, I dearly hope so."

The Prime Minister put his hand on his shoulder. "So do I, Donald, so do I. My son Hugh is going to be with him.

"Enough of your worrying, Donald, really." The Prime Minister was in an incredibly buoyant mood. "I have a surprise for you, Donald. I've arranged for a demonstration."

"Oh? And what might it be that I am to see demonstrated?"

"Well, by the most incredible good fortune, an American citizen was in Ottawa trying to sell a remarkable new weapon. I had General Middleton look at it and he was, well, very impressed. Better yet, it comes with a practised expert who is willing to travel west and train a crew to use it."

"Does this remarkable weapon have a name?"

"It's called a Gatling gun. Fires bullets at a simply remarkable speed I understand."

Smith smiled in amusement. He already knew quite a bit about the Gatling gun. Could be the gun that would win the West, he thought.

Lieutenant Arthur Howard was a former cavalry officer retired from the U.S. Army. He had been the first man trained to use the amazing gun and it was his pride and joy. He did not actually work for the company that had invented it, but travelled around demonstrating the magnificent weapon on behalf of its owners. Now he was standing in front of the Canadian troopers selected to be trained as gunners. Also in attendance were Donald Smith, Sir John A. Macdonald, and General Frederick Middleton.

Before him was a great wooden crate with an American flag on it. He opened one end of the crate and he and two other men rolled the great gun out. It had multiple rifle barrels arranged like a sheaf of metal rods, a handle that was cranked by hand, and a stand and wheels that allowed it to be positioned and aimed. He lined it up to face a large wooden target about twenty-five yards away.

Lieutenant Howard loaded the gun, explaining various points as he did so to his audience. Then as a hush fell over the crowd, he stepped up dramatically to the handle, braced himself, and began firing. In less than a minute the target was rivetted with at least two hundred bullet holes. He stopped and looked at the faces of the onlookers.

164

"Good God," Smith gasped.

Sir John nodded. Even he preferred such a weapon to be used on a wooden target. "You think it might even Middleton's odds against 'Métis' warfare?"

"I daresay," Smith replied.

17

The Beginning of the End

Let him who does not know what war is, go to war.

Spanish proverb

"God save me from leading any more volunteers into combat." Major Crozier and his defeated troops were marching back to Prince Albert from Duck Lake. The town was full of refugees from the outlying farms and small settlements. He looked about him and knew that there would be more. There was nothing to do but abandon the far-flung Hudson's Bay posts and remain in Prince Albert. Troops were coming in six weeks, reinforcements from Regina in three—two, depending on who you believed, and if they were able to make it at all. Crozier sent a telegram to Ottawa informing them of his decision to defend Prince Albert. It was the last telegram anyone sent, because Gabriel Dumont and Métis horsemen shot down the wires.

"No more messages for them, eh Pierre?"
"This is good target practice."
"Now we send out our scouts," Dumont declared. "We have to know where their army is, even if they don't." They all laughed and returned to Batoche.
Old Ouellette was sitting on a stump, making something from scraps. Louis looked on with interest.

"What's he doing?" asked Dumont.

Louis looked up into Gabriel's eyes. "I am a prophet, a messiah. I need something special for my altar."

Gabriel looked into Louis' face—his expression was almost "sweet" and he seemed benevolent and happy. Gabriel gestured toward old Ouellette. "If that's what you say you need, he'll make it."

Louis frowned and caught Gabriel's eyes again in his gaze. "What do you say we do, Gabriel?"

Gabriel laughed. "I say I should dynamite the railway!"

Louis' face was white, questioning. "Do you have doubts, Gabriel?"

He shrugged. "About what? What we are fighting for? Hell, no!" He paused and touched Louis' hand. "Forgive me, Louis. I know my words offend you sometimes."

Louis persisted. "I mean doubts about me? More than any of the others, you must believe in me . . . in what I am . . . in what I do for God and his people everywhere."

Gabriel looked down kindly at Louis. "I believe God wants us to live as we are, strong like the Indian, crazy like the French, free to roam like the buffalo on land that belongs to no man, but to all men."

Louis sank to his knees. "Oh Gabriel, you do understand! Yes to all the oppressed people, the land is theirs —ours. I am God's holy instrument to bring this about. Starting here in Batoche. Even, even if we must all fight with our lives."

Dumont nodded. "Louis, are you sure God—or his prophet, Louis Riel—doesn't want me to blow up the railway?"

"Not now." The simplicity of his answer somehow seemed to make sense. Perhaps, Gabriel thought, we should wait until they reached a certain place and blow up two parts of the railway. Then they could go neither forward nor backward. Ah, five thousand men and three hundred horses, trapped, with their band of steel blown to bits.

Louis and old Ouellette went to nail up the new shrine on the tree and then Louis ordered the church bells rung for a meeting. Father Ritchot came scurrying out of the church as the bells pealed. Métis from all over the Saskatchewan gathered as Louis moved to the steps to be heard.

"Hear me, my brothers! The Canadian troops are coming to Batoche! They come to challenge us as a nation. Are we a nation?"

Métis and Indian alike cheered in unison.

"Will the Métis take up arms to protect their nation when it is invaded?"

Again the crowd cheered. Gabriel looked up with pride to Louis. His eyes held the crowd, his voice and the words he spoke rang in their ears. They wanted to hear these words, no, they *needed* desperately to hear these words.

Father Ritchot fought his way through the crowd to Louis' side. "Louis! For God's sake . . . !

Louis turned on him almost savagely. "Yes! For God's sake, we fight for what is ours and for what God wants us to be!"

Father Ritchot offered a challenge. "Listen, everyone! This is not the way! Your priests . . . the church . . . all of us are opposed to this violence."

Louis turned on Ritchot. A crazed and demonic look came into his eyes that Gabriel had not seen for many years, not since . . . Quickly he blotted the memory out.

"There is no church!" His words rang as the bells had pealed only moments before. "Rome has fallen! There are no priests . . . only men who believe in us and men who are our enemies!" Louis suddenly seized Father Ritchot's arm. "This man is an enemy! Arrest him!"

Father Ritchot stepped backward. The old man's face was pale. He looked into the wild eyes of a man he had baptized as an infant, a man he had nurtured like a son and taught to read. He looked pleadingly into his face, looking for reason, and what he saw was neither recognition nor reason.

"Arrest this man!" Louis shouted again.

Pierre shifted restlessly on his horse. He whispered into Dumont's ear, "Gabriel, he's gone mad!"

The crowd was silent now. Dumont seized Pierre's arm and hissed back at him, "Never, ever, say that again, do you hear me? Not to anyone!" He released him and shouted to the crowd. "Arrest him! Be quick about it! We have to get more arms to hunt fresh Canadian buffalo with! For God! For Louis Riel! And for the Métis nation!" He raised his rifle toward the sky and a thunderous war whoop broke from the horsemen.

When the clamor had died down, Gabriel moved off with his men and began assigning tasks. Trenches, ammunition, food, all were a priority. He dispatched messengers and set up his own "telegraph." Lastly, he considered the children of Batoche. They must have somewhere to hide, somewhere out of the battle, and he put the Métis women to organizing it.

"Our time will pass swiftly," Pierre said. "They will be on us before we know it."

Dumont nodded. "We will have warning."

Pierre began shovelling. "Gabriel, this is not our way to fight—"

"Louis said we must start in Batoche."

Pierre looked around. "Well, the ground is not bad, higher here than down there."

Gabriel reached up and felt the bandage still on his head. His thoughts returned to the vision of Louis praying over him.

Pierre noticed him. "How's your head? That *anglais* bullet near Duck Lake give you a near miss."

"It's all right," he assured him. "Just a flesh wound."

Pierre smiled. "We thought you gone to meet your Maker."

"I don't intend to go that way," Gabriel said with conviction.

"You're a lucky sonofabitch if you get to choose."

"You'll see, Pierre. I get to choose."

Pierre leaned on the shovel and looked at Gabriel. "I think you should go talk with Louis now. This is not our way to fight. We fight on horseback, we run them into a trap, move in on them. This is *anglais* way to fight. We can't win this way!"

Gabriel shrugged. "I'll talk to him, he'll talk to me—we'll end up here. Make that deep enough to hide yourself in."

With that, Dumont walked off. Of course Pierre was right. But there was some time left.

He found Louis at his desk, writing. "You writing your own bible?"

Louis looked up. He wore that tired, intense look again, the look that spoke a thousand words. Gabriel resolved that this time he would get Louis out in time. No more arrests, no more asylums.

"It's not a bible, it's a revelation," Louis declared. "It's a companion to my plan for this territory."

Gabriel listened, as he always did.

"We're going to have a new church. I want Bishop Bourget to be Pope."

"Bishop Bourget?" Gabriel gasped. "Louis, I want you to get some rest. You need to sleep."

"I have too much work to do."

Gabriel looked at the blank pieces of paper strewn across the top of the desk. He closed his eyes for a moment, not quite sure what to say.

"Louis, you must rest now. Your work will wait until tomorrow."

"No, my revelation is coming now. I must write it down. God directs my pen so I can write."

"No, Louis. The men will need you tomorrow. They need your words and your prayers. You must be rested. A leader must have energy."

Louis looked into Gabriel's eyes and acquiesced. "Of course, they need me and I must be there." Louis allowed Gabriel to lead him to his bed and cover him with the blankets.

"Rest, Louis, rest."

"My God it's muddy here!" General Middleton was addressing Lieutenant Pearce, his First Officer.

Pearce looked down into a sea of mud. "It's not very pleasant country, is it, sir?"

Middleton swatted at a mosquito. "God no, even the filthy bugs are hostile."

Middleton spread out over his horse. He was a portly man with white hair and a long white waxed mustache. He wore his dress uniform and sported a chest full of medals.

"How are they holding up?" Middleton asked, pointing ahead to the long line of trudging men.

"They're Canadians, sir. Volunteers. Not like the kind of troops we have at home."

"By God, it's worse than bloody India! Mud, flies that eat you, mosquitoes, rain, freezing nights. A man needs the British Army to conduct war in a country like this. What time is it, Pearce?"

"Nearly six, sir. It'll be getting dark soon. This territory is rather bad, sir. I don't like the ravines on either side of the river much."

"It's the fastest way, Pearce. We'll stop in a while. I want to divide the men."

"Divide the men, sir?"

"Yes," Middleton pulled himself up and shook his head. "I want two battalions. One will travel on the left side of the river and the other on the right. And why do you mention the ravines?"

"I was just thinking of Custer, sir."

Middleton gave Pearce a withering look. "Custer who?"

"Sorry, General. It's just that we don't know the terrain all that well."

"We have a map, Pearce, and we have scouts—three excellent guides."

Pearce nodded.

Suddenly shots rang through the air—they seemed to be coming from all directions.

"We're totally exposed!" Sergeant William Franklin yelled behind them.

Middleton and Pearce made for the nearest wagon. "Tip that blasted thing over," Middleton ordered. "Get your head down, Pearce, before one of those savage scalp hunters shoots it off!"

An order went down the line, men ran for cover, and the horses went into a panic.

"We've got casualties already, General!"

"Oh course we have casualties, you greenhorn nitwit! That's what happens when you get hit by a bullet! Christ! Where the hell are they? I can't see anything anywhere!"

"I think that's the idea, sir."

"Thank you, Mr. Pearce. And when this is over, you must tell me about your friend, Mr. Custer."

"*General* Custer, sir."

Pearce reloaded and peered out into the semidarkness. The lengthening shadows of twilight made it very difficult to see. He knew only that bullets were still buzzing through the air and killing and wounding his men. Bullets from invisible rifles.

Napoleon Nault grinned over at Gabriel Dumont. "We're getting a lot of *anglais* buffalo, eh?"

Gabriel smiled broadly. "The *anglais* General 'Middlegrosse,' he is not too smart."

They laughed at the joke. " 'Middlegrosse' is a good name for him, Gabriel."

172

"Well, he looks like the ripe pear before she falls off the tree."

"We shake the tree, eh?"

"We're ready," Pierre said. "It's not our kind of fighting," Tremblay added. "We teach them something, but I think they get us sooner or later."

"We'll show them Métis courage," Gabriel said. "Then maybe we get lucky, we get Louis and get the hell out of this country!"

Two thousand miles away, Bishop Ignace Bourget sat behind his desk with his hands folded. Father Charles McWilliams stood before him, holding a sheaf of papers.

The Bishop looked up at McWilliams. "Have you come to the part where he names me Pope, to preside over his new religion?"

"No, Your Grace, I'm still at the part where he's describing the religion . . . renaming the days of the week, the countries of the world . . . polygamy. Let's see, Saturday is to be the Lord's day of rest . . . Yes, yes! Here it is. 'And Bishop Bourget is to be . . .'"

"I *know* what it says, Father!" The Bishop's tone was impatient. "The implications are embarrassing and frightening."

McWilliams looked up from the paper. "It's as if Louis had this bottled up for years and it all finally exploded. It must have grown in him during all those years of exile."

Bourget looked past McWilliams. "My concern for him is deep, Father, but my concern for *all* French Catholics is deeper. Here in Quebec we will be forced to draw closer together and become more protective of our language and our religion—of each other. I fear we will gradually grow more isolated from the rest of Canada. In the West, our gains could be in jeopardy."

McWilliams studied the Bishop's face. "I hope you are wrong, Your Grace. I'm certain that Father Ritchot has great strength. I am sure he will protect the people and the faith."

"You are naive, Father." The Bishop's voice was now more sad than angry.

"Perhaps," McWilliams agreed. He did not know himself. He thought for a moment and then added, "Even if Father Ritchot cannot handle things, there is your friend Charles Nolin. Is he not in Ottawa now?"

Bishop Bourget nodded. After a pause he said, "I am not sure that Mr. Nolin will be much help. He feathers his own nest and divides the Métis. A house divided against itself cannot stand long." The Bishop's tone was sad. ". . . Either politically or religiously," he added.

The five men of the Prime Minister's inner cabinet all sat at one end of the long mahogany table. Sir John sat at the head and chaired the informal meeting. On the left side of the table sat Charles Nolin. The small group seemed dwarfed by the size of the room and the length of the table. Pipe smoke rose into the air as the men relaxed against the plush, red velvet upholstery of the Victorian chairs.

Nolin, his long dark hair drawn back in Indian fashion, leaned forward. "I wanted you to know, Mr. Prime Minister, there are some of us who are Métis *and* Canadians. We find no conflict in being both."

The Prime Minister did not look up from his papers as he answered. "You reassure us, Mr. Nolin."

Nolin cleared his throat. "There *are* some claims I have . . ." He shuffled some of his own papers in order to appear more businesslike. "Some papers I sent that are still unanswered. The people involved . . . we're loyal Canadians in a hostile place. Any help . . ." His sentence trailed off as the Prime Minister looked up and stared at him. "Thank you for sharing your first-hand report on the territory, and your most helpful insight into the personality of Riel."

The Prime Minister rose abruptly and motioned to the others that the meeting was at an end. Nolin rose too, and glancing around the room somewhat nervously, gathered his papers and mumbled, "Yes . . . well, thank you all again."

Sir John consulted his gold timepiece to avoid looking directly into Nolin's anxious eyes. "I'll look into your claims, Mr. Nolin. You'll hear from us shortly."

Nolin nodded and quietly passed through the great oak doors.

A. T. Bennett looked at Sir John. "Second thoughts about sending Middleton and the troops, Sir John?"

The Prime Minister had been allowing his mind to wander, and Bennett's question snapped him back to reality. "What? No . . . no, of course not. Nolin's an opportunist . . . smells a chance to improve his own position. I'm an opportunist too. I've used this to move the railroad farther west. But discounting all that, everything I hear now convinces me we could have talked till doomsday with Riel and still have gotten nowhere. No, Riel came back to Canada meaning to have a fight and by God we'll give it to him! Anything less and we might as well fold up the country and parcel it out to whoever would take it. What I did was right. I'm more convinced of it than ever."

Bennett nodded his agreement. "One has to put down any and all separationist ideas before they grow."

"Yes. By taking a strong hand now we spare future generations of Canadians any such problems. This will remain one nation. Now no one will ever question the resolve of the federal government again!"

18

Batoche: 1885

And we are here as on a darkling plain
Swept with confused alarms of struggle and flight,
Where ignorant armies clash by night.

Mathew Arnold

"Company A: eight dead, forty-one wounded. Company B: five dead, sixteen wounded. Company C: twelve dead, thirty-two wounded." Lieutenant Pearce read from his preliminary casualty list, paused, and then added, "We also have 246 men who are suffering from dysentery, flu, and scarlet fever."

Middleton shook his head in dismay. "And do we have any such careful statistics on the enemy?"

Pearce withdrew a piece of paper from under his official casualty report. "Best estimates are there were about a hundred of them. We seem to have killed two."

"*Seem* to have killed?" The General was obviously irritated.

"Well, sir, we found two bodies. They might have taken more with them, and we have no way of knowing about their wounded."

The General's face was red. "This is ridiculous! That's a ridiculous report! We are quite obviously underrating these natives. I was in the battle myself you know."

Pearce lowered his head. "Yes sir, I know."

"There was a large number—a very large number, in my own estimate, at least five hundred. Now write that in the report!"

"Yes, sir." Pearce looked at his paper and sighed. Lieutenant Andrews, a young Canadian officer, interjected. "Excuse me, sir, they had dug trenches high above the hills that made it impossible to see them."

Wilson, a volunteer captain from Red River, looked at Pearce, Andrews, and the General. Everything in his own background and experience told him they were wrong. "Those were not trenches, they were buffalo tracks, sir. The Métis know these hills, our men didn't have . . ."

General Middleton was angry and exasperated. "Where are you from, Captain?" he snapped.

"Manitoba, sir."

The General turned on all of them, his eyes moving from one to the other. "I asked for a report, not a book filled with this and that! Irrelevancies! Horseshit! You go tell those green Canadian troopers that professional English officers are going to lead them to Batoche whether they're ready or not." The General's voice grew angrier with each word. "We will meet with this devil, Louis Riel, and we will beat the hell out of these savages—with the Canadians or without! Do you understand, gentlemen?"

The three men straightened up and saluted. "Yes, sir," they snapped in unison.

The General allowed his body and his facial expression to relax. "I have scheduled the Battle of Batoche for eight a.m., day after tomorrow. I intend to keep to my schedule."

The three young officers looked at each other. Each felt the other's uneasiness at this pronouncement.

"And," the General added, "tell that blasted American, Howard, to get his gun ready."

Gabriel Dumont and his fifty buffalo hunters rode into Batoche. The Métis who remained behind were digging more trenches. Louis was moving about silently inspecting them, and blessing the men as he spoke with each one. He stopped abruptly when he saw Gabriel. Crucifix in hand, he ran over to him.

"You have brought me my victory?" His face was contorted with excitement. Gabriel looked down into the tired, but strangely glowing eyes of his friend. "Your prayers, Louis, made it happen." Louis smiled and crossed himself.

"Go rest, Louis," he said softly. "They are close now, soon the men will need you constantly. Sleep now. I'll see to the trenches."

Louis pulled him aside and whispered in his ear. "God has spoken to me. The trenches must be built toward the church."

Gabriel looked at him and then looked toward the church. "Why?" he asked.

"Because that is the plan I have received. It is the will of God." Louis' voice was intense.

Gabriel looked into the glowing eyes and nodded his agreement. "Yes, that is how we will dig them, but only if you go now and rest." Gabriel walked among the digging men and paused when he came to Lépine. "No. It must turn that way . . . up toward the church, and be sure it is deep enough."

Lépine looked into the eyes of the man he trusted most in the world. "Gabriel, you are a practical man. If you are hungry, you eat. If it rains, you find cover. When the enemy comes, do you pray or fight?"

Gabriel looked at the terrain. "I pray that I can fight," he answered simply.

"You have seen how many there are," Lépine continued. "You have seen their guns. There will be no stopping them here."

Gabriel looked into Lépine's eyes. There was a finality in his voice as he said, "Then make sure you pray *before* you fight!"

Gabriel looked at Louis' shrine. He himself had a plan, a plan by which he hoped to save the Métis. The way the trenches were being built was not right. But what did it matter? There was an escape route, and moreover, he hoped to be engaging the enemy head on and from the sides when Poundmaker and his Cree warriors attacked from the rear. It was a good plan. It would succeed. In any case, the idiot "Middlegrosse" was dividing his men. He would be fighting with half a force. The other half would have to go miles downstream before they could cross the Saskatchewan River.

Old Ouellette approached him. "This is all the ammunition we could find," he said.

Dumont looked at the stocks. "We need more metal." He motioned to Lépine. "The two of you come with me."

They tore the wooden barriers off the door of the church and Father Ritchot looked up expectantly.

"You are going to release me? You have all come to your senses?" Gabriel looked at him and shook his head. He walked to the side and with a loud crash pulled the stove out of the wall. "Excuse me, Father." He said it with mock politeness.

"Here is your metal, Ouellette." Lépine dragged the stove from the church. Gabriel looked at Ouellette and motioned toward Father Ritchot. "My apologies, Father. Close him up again!"

Father Ritchot went back to the little place he had fixed for himself. He tore some of the black bread from the loaf. "At least they feed me," he thought. He poured some of the sacramental wine into a glass and, mixing it with water, took a large gulp. "Something has to happen soon," he said aloud. "This cannot continue forever." He covered himself with one of the blankets he had piled on the floor to make a sleeping place. The wine filled his body with warmth and numbed his senses. It didn't matter, he reasoned, there was simply nothing he could do. Gradually he fell into a deep sleep.

The shot cracked through the morning air, rapidly followed by another and another. Father Ritchot sat bolt upright, then ran to the small window. He squinted.

He could see no Métis, but over the ridge he saw troops spreading out in formation. He crossed himself. He did not know whether he was sad or relieved, fearful or relaxed. The drama was unfolding before him and he felt that he was about to witness a major battle. The whole scene seemed somehow unreal.

The first round of bullets from the Gatling gun ripped through the front of the church. Father Ritchot jumped from his position near the window and crawled along the floor behind one of the pews.

Riel turned to Dumont in horror. "Father Ritchot! He's still inside."

Dumont turned to Napoleon. "Quick, open the back door. Let him out!"

Up on the hill, Middleton shook Howard from behind. "That's a bloody church, you fool!"

Howard stopped the gun. "General, the position's wrong. I can't get an angle from up here."

"Well, don't fire that damned thing until you can!" Middleton wiped his brow.

"There's someone coming with a white flag, General."

Middleton peered into the sunlight. He saw the black-frocked figure running toward his troops. "Hold your fire!" His command moved along the line.

Father Ritchot ran as fast as his long cassock would allow. "May God tell them not to shoot, may God tell them not to shoot," he mumbled to himself as he ran. He collapsed in front of Lieutenant Pearce, who helped him to his feet. Ritchot was shaking from head to foot. He looked blankly at General Middleton. "God told them not to shoot," he said breathlessly. Middleton looked at him with disdain. "*I* told them not to shoot," he said haughtily.

Ritchot turned toward where he knew the Métis were hidden and shouted at the top of his lungs, "Louis Riel, may God have mercy on your soul!" Then he sat down in exhaustion. "He's mad," he said aloud. He looked around at the guns, the artillery, and the Gatling gun that pointed toward the church. His mind could not take in the number of troops he saw.

Middleton stepped back and signalled for Andrews. "Take this man behind the lines and interrogate him." Anderson obediently led Father Ritchot away, mumbling.

Suddenly, on the left, a group of soldiers attempted to move forward, but shots rang out and two fell to the ground. Pearce ordered them to pull back.

"What the hell do you think you're doing?" Middleton yelled.

"Our position is bad, sir! We've got to pull back!"

Middleton snapped at him. "The hell you say! I am conducting this battle, Lieutenant Pearce!"

"Yes, sir." Pearce moved off.

"What's your range with that gun now, Howard?"

He shrugged. "Hard to tell at this angle, General. We'll just have to try and see." Howard cranked the handle of the Gatling and the bullets spewed forth, ripping up the ground and kicking up puffs of dirt in a line. "I have to be closer, sir," he said. "Our position, the angle, it's not right."

Middleton surveyed the whole scene. "Pearce!" he bellowed over the sound of incessant rifle fire.

"Yes, sir?" Pearce was crouched behind a rock.

"Order sixty men to charge that line!" Middleton pointed off to the left.

"I can't see a line, sir. I can't see anything." Middleton narrowed his eyes. "God damn it! You don't have to see it to know it's there. Charge that line!"

Pearce ordered the charge and again men fell in all directions. The lucky ones crawled back on their stomachs.

Middleton stood up. "Fall back. Fall back!" Then he moved behind the lines. "Get some men to build some pallisades! Over there!" He motioned toward an open area. "Regroup!" he ordered.

Lieutenant Pearce looked around him at the dead and wounded and made another casualty count.

Middleton stood with his hands on this hips. "If they have time, we have time," he said to Pearce. "We'll continue to harass them, make them use up their ammunition. "We'll need the pallisades tonight."

Pearce nodded. At least Middleton realized now it wasn't going to be as easy as he thought.

"Sir, I don't think they're used to fighting this way."

"What way?" Middleton queried.

"In position, sir. I think we should try a full charge."

Middleton shook his head. "We'll loose too many men. We'll wait for the other battalion to join us." Middleton rubbed his chin. He wondered where the silly bastards were. They should have been here by this time.

Sporadic gunfire continued throughout the day. Riel passed intermittently among the trenches, bearing the great crucifix and praying. "God is helping us, God is helping us," he would cry. His eyes glowed as he looked at Gabriel. "They are not coming, we are winning," he cried.

Gabriel nodded. He thought only of the dwindling supply of ammunition. Twenty-seven *anglais* buffalo, he thought. Four Métis dead, including Napoleon's wife. Dumont did not like the gun that fired rapidly.

Lieutenant Pearce entered General Middleton's command tent, safe behind the walls of the stockade.

"Begging your pardon, sir." He extended a bullet toward the General.

Taking it, Middleton turned it slowly under the light of the oil lamp. "It's a bullet from a Snider-Enfield."

Pearce straightened up. "It was removed from one of our troops."

Middleton put it down carefully. "I didn't know the half-breeds had Snider-Enfields."

Pearce leaned over toward Middleton. "They don't, sir. They're so short of ammunition they're digging our bullets out of the ground and shooting them back at us.

182

Sir, one of the Canadian volunteers, a lieutenant, says he knows these people. He's been against them before. He believes if we rush them, they'd fall apart."

Middleton rose, smoothing out his uniform as he did so. "Lieutenant, I want to clean up this mess with as little loss of life as possible."

"Sir, he says . . ."

"Thank you, Pearce. And now I would like to eat my dinner in peace."

Pearce knew when he was beaten. "There's just one more thing, sir."

Middleton turned wearily. "And what is that, Pearce?"

"The Prime Minister's son, sir, young Hugh Macdonald. He died of scarlet fever earlier this evening."

Middleton shook his head. "Wretched disease. See to it his father is notified."

"Yes, General." Pearce backed out of the tent and moved among the exhausted troops. Captain Wilson came up to him anxiously. "What'd he say?" Pearce shrugged. "He said he'll do it his way." Wilson shook his head. "Pompous old fool!" Pearce nodded his agreement. "Shh, shh. He'd have you for lunch if that got back to him."

At six a.m. the first light of dawn began to appear. Silently in the semidarkness of the early morning light the women and children began leaving Batoche, following the route Gabriel had planned for them. Louis carried his crucifix. His face was dead white, but his eyes glowed. Gabriel whispered to him, "It's better that they're out of this."

Marguerite carried one of Louis' children in her arms, while the others clung to her skirts and followed silently. Louis walked beside her. "We've been like strangers, I've had no time . . ." Marguerite reached up and stroked the back of his head with her free hand. "We'll be together soon, Louis," she said simply. "Whatever you must do is God's will."

Louis stopped and looked around him. "If the sun shines today, we will win; if the clouds come, we will lose."

Gabriel took his arm. "They will be safe now. We go back." Louis kissed the baby and squeezed his wife's arm. "I must go and do as God has directed me." Marguerite nodded bravely.

Dumont watched the women and children of Batoche leave. His eyes followed Marguerite. She is more Indian than French, he thought.

Dumont turned and scanned the horizon. The Cree, Poundmaker. Where were they? He could not know the answer, he knew only that time was fast running out.

Middleton addressed his officers as the sun broke over the horizon.

"There will be a signal when we are in position to commence firing. Then we will advance in the usual manner and systematically move down into the village while still covering ourselves. You officers on the ridges, do not move your men until you see my signal."

The men dispersed and Pearce moved off with Wilson. "Another day of harassment," he said sarcastically. Wilson shook his head. "Maybe, maybe." Pearce did not like the way he said "maybe," but there were just some things he did not want to know about.

Meanwhile, in Batoche, Louis moved among the men, blessing them and holding high his cross. "God has blessed us with the sun." He pointed toward the horizon. "It is the sign God has given me. This day we will be victorious!"

Dumont saw the faces of the men. Louis always galvanized them, made a unit of them. They moved quietly to take their positions among the others as the troops again fanned out in their rigid formations.

Old Ouellette looked at Gabriel. "I'm ninety-four," he said proudly, loading his rifle. "And you're still the best," Gabriel answered. "When the time comes,

Gabriel," said Ouellette, looking into Dumont's eyes, "do not look back. I will cover you. I won't live much longer anyway. This is *my* chosen way." Gabriel smiled at his old friend. "Thank you. I hope I will not have to take you up on your offer."

Ominously, the wind began blowing from the west and clouds began to appear over the ridge. A sudden spring storm approached to meet the rising sun. Gabriel shook his head. So, he thought, this is the way our world ends.

If either Gabriel Dumont or General Middleton could have surveyed the total scene, the deciding battle at Batoche might have gone differently. Mid-way up one rise stood the small prairie church so recently occupied by the prisoner, Father Ritchot. Its doors, windows, and walls were shattered from the previous day's fighting, and heavy damage had been inflicted by the rapid fire of the Gatling gun, which had riddled the entire front of the church with holes.

Beyond the church on the rise of the hill was Batoche. Its buildings were scattered halfway down the far side of the hill, but its main centre was on the top of the rise. Beyond the hill occupied by the village were thick woods, woods that provided a hiding place for the women and children as well as an escape route for the Métis fighters.

Rows of deep trenches lined and protected the front of the village, both below the church where Louis had instructed them dug, and above, where Dumont had arranged for additional trenches. The trenches were dug to resemble the natural buffalo runs so often used by Métis fighters. They consisted of long, deep furrows partially or almost completely covered by tall gass. From such vantage points the riflemen were able to see, but not be seen. They could pick off attackers as they moved forward and came within range of their hidden rifles.

General Middleton arranged his troops in the classical

pattern. It was a system not much different from the one originated by Alexander the Great at the battle of Arbela, three centuries before the birth of Christ. It remained the standard pattern for fixed battles until the end of the nineteenth century.

General Middleton's five thousand troops were deployed in a right and left phalanx, with a strong centre line joining the two. The centre line called for heavily armed infantry in such close order that their fire and protective cover overlapped. They were preceded by cannon and Gatling gun fire. This was the strong frontal force which, as it edged forward, moved in co-ordination with the right and left phalanx, each of which could be gradually tightened or expanded if necessary. The strategy was to enclose the enemy in a gradually decreasing three-sided unfinished square. Middleton believed that flanking fire would protect the centre line advance, thus limiting casualties. And he counted heavily on the Gatling gun to cover the centre advance, reasoning that its extraordinary storm of bullets would stun the Métis and limit their ability to reload or accurately hit the oncoming sea of men.

Middleton did not know, and would never have admitted, that his force outnumbered the Métis by more than ten to one. He had decided to fight a cautious battle, to follow a classical plan, designed to wear out the Métis completely. It was for those reasons he had so carefully briefed his men the night before—no one was to advance without the signal.

"What the hell's the matter with him?" Captain Wilson was mounted and waiting on the far ridge but he could see no sign of Middleton's signal. The artillery boomed and the Gatling gun fired steadily. There was rifle fire from virtually every direction. Wilson peered at the Métis position. He could see that they were hemmed in and he watched them break ranks and begin to crawl out of their holes to run for more distant cover.

He looked at Middleton. The fat old fool still ordered no rush.

"To hell with him!" he shouted to his men. He raised his arm and gave the signal to charge. They rode hard and fast, firing as they went. The others saw him and thought Middleton had given the order. The force was joined by the other officers and men. "Attack!" Wilson shouted. "Attack!"

Middleton stood with Pearce. All he could see was riders and riflemen attacking. "Those damn fools!" he muttered weakly.

Dumont ran low and fast to reach his horse, knowing the battle was now lost. Ouellette held his position and covered him. He glanced around at the confusion and the retreating men, while Louis stood stark still as the troops began overrunning the forward trenches, mesmerized by the horror. Low in the saddle, Gabriel rode up and lifted Louis onto his horse. He made for the woods he knew so well, for the hiding place he had prepared weeks ago. Louis held on desperately to Gabriel's waist as they escaped the scene of blood, bullets, and rifle fire.

Some of the others had gotten away too. Dumont knew that each man had his own place to escape to, his own plan. The soldiers could not follow all of them. He and Louis would be the main targets of any search. Time was terribly important.

When he reached the well-hidden and secluded cave, he dismounted. Inside were different clothes, fresh ammunition, and food. Supplies for the trip south. Two fresh horses grazed where he had left them.

He turned to Louis who stood stiffly against a tree. "Fresh horses, we head due south and in two days we're across the border and safe."

Louis dropped to his knees and began praying.

Gabriel touched his shoulder. "Soon the soldiers will be all through these woods and we'll be shot on sight."

Louis continued to pray. Tears ran down his face and he shook all over. "Louis!" Gabriel's voice took on a sense of command, of urgency. "Louis! You and God talk to each other twenty-four hours a day! Let him catch his breath a minute while you listen to me!"

Louis turned and looked up into Gabriel's eyes.

"Do you know what they'll do if they capture you?"

Louis' eyes were tranquil. His voice was low and showed his resignation. "I know that if I run I deprive all this of any meaning."

Gabriel looked at him sadly. "We'll stay then."

Louis stood up and took Gabriel's hands. "Gabriel, my good disciple. I must make that last familiar walk myself. But we shall meet again."

Gabriel saw that Louis would not be moved. "Louis," he said. "Please . . ."

But Louis turned and walked off into the woods alone.

Gabriel spurred his horse and headed south. He gripped his saddle horn with one hand and bit his lip. He had gotten Louis into this by bringing him back. He did not like to leave him, but he knew Louis would not come. He thought of the great Indian chief who, when faced with the death of his people and his own captivity, simply willed himself to die on the spot. Louis would let them kill him because he believed he had to die.

They would look at Louis Riel and call him mad. They would see themselves in him and they would hate him for that.

19

The End of a Dream

Martyrs, my friend, have to choose between being forgotten, mocked, or used. As for being understood, never.

Albert Camus

"Of course you can make a case out of it, Osler. "You're the Minister of Justice." The Prime Minister's voice was impatient. Osler was bringing on Sir John's sometime annoyance with the legal profession.

"Sir John, it is a difficult case in which to establish a charge."

The Prime Minister rose and walked around the front of his desk to face Osler. "The charge is treason, man. I want him taken to Regina. I want him tried and I expect him to be convicted!"

Osler shuffled his papers nervously. "He's an American citizen. He took out papers in Montana. The Americans won't . . ."

Macdonald slammed his fist down on the desk. "That didn't stop him from leading a rebellion in Canada! The voters demand action!"

Donald Smith stood in the corner quietly, but now he felt forced to say something. "The French look on him as one of them. With an election coming, it could alienate Quebec."

The Prime Minister stepped back. "You think I don't realize that? And if he's set free, it will alienate English Canada." Macdonald brought his fist down hard against his hand. His tone was one of exasperation. "Must every issue, large or small, provincial or federal, become a test of the very identity of this country?"

Smith interjected. "It would seem so, Sir John, it would seem so."

The Prime Minister shook his head. "Pray, gentlemen, that we will mature and that future generations will be spared such destructive spectacles."

Osler fidgeted. He couldn't stand this kind of philosophizing. It did not clarify his objectives at all. The voters were not his concern—the law was his concern.

"Perhaps a lesser offence," he suggested.

"Treason," the Prime Minister said emphatically. Osler acquiesced. "Yes, treason." He turned to Sir John and to Smith. "It's going to be a difficult case. I must go now."

Sir John straightened himself up. "Thank you for coming, Osler, it's always nice to have a meeting of minds."

Smith shook his head. "God knows what they'll plead. I'm certain they'll have to defend him—the church just has too much at stake."

Sir John looked evenly at Smith. "Yes. Riel's going to cause a great public outcry. Half the country will want to save his soul and the other half will want to see him swing."

"And you, Sir John?"

"I don't care if he hangs, if he spends his life in prison, or if they send him off to some mental institution. Whatever makes the most voters happy!"

"That seems a bit callous!"

"Nonsense, Donald. I believe in majority rule."

Some miles distant in Montreal, Bishop Bourget was pacing in his office. Demonstrations! Special prayer services! Even special masses! The knock on the door startled him. "Enter!" He must watch himself. He needed more rest—this thing was getting worse every day.

Father McWilliams entered with a tall distinguished-looking man. "I have brought Monsieur François Lemieux, as you wished, Your Grace. He is the best defence attorney in all Quebec."

The Bishop looked up at McWilliams impatiently. "If he were not the best, I would not have sent for him!"

Bourget held out his hand to Lemieux. "Forgive me. Riel was . . . is very close to me."

"I can sense your concern, Your Grace."

"Please take a chair. Let us discuss Louis. We must find a way to save him." Bourget slumped into the chair behind his desk and covered his eyes with his hands. His words were slow, painful. "Louis Riel *must* be saved."

"There are many issues, Your Grace." Lemieux opened his briefcase.

The Bishop looked up. "If they can extinguish this French voice in the wilderness, it will be snuffed out throughout the country. I dreamed once of a Catholic New France in the West. So did Louis Riel, once. Once we two were dreamers. Perhaps we shared a foolish dream, perhaps . . ." His voice trailed off.

"I have been studying the case, Your Grace. The man is obviously well intentioned, but very ill. I think the perfect compromise might be a plea of insanity."

Bishop Bourget looked into Lemieux's face. "Yes," he said, "yes, insanity! He is quite insane."

McWilliams watched the two carefully, but with contempt. He knew then that he must go west to be with Louis.

The courtroom in Regina was small and crowded with as many people as could be packed into the room. Father Ritchot sat nervously tapping his fingers together. Charles Nolin sat next to him, looking very placid and self-satisfied. The chairs were straight-backed and uncomfortable. The walls of the tiny room were bare, save for the portrait of Her Majesty which hung above the elevated desk reserved for the judge. Two tables, reserved for the defence and the prosecuters, were located in front of the judge's desk on a level equal to that of the spectators. The far side of the room was lined with three rows of benches for the press, and opposite them sat the jury.

Louis was brought in to the crowded room by a guard, his hands chained. As he entered, his head was filled with the whispers of the spectators. François Lemieux was already seated and he rose as Louis approached.

Osler sat at the other table with three advisers, his papers piled in front of him.

Louis turned, and his eyes fell on Dr. Roy. He turned to Lemieux. "What's he doing here?"

Lemieux put his finger to his mouth to gesture for silence. The judge had entered and was making his way to the bench. He had white hair, which contrasted with his black robes and bright blue eyes, and he was a heavy-set man.

Louis barely heard the court called to order or the preliminary statements. He scribbled on pieces of paper, trying to get his thoughts in order.

Osler stood to make his opening statement, his voice harsh, sarcastic. " 'The prophet of Saskatchewan' was the cry under which his poor dupes were supposed to rally . . . Gentlemen of the jury, you will be satisfied before this case is over that it is not a matter brought about by any wrongs on the part of these poor primitive people . . ." He turned and pointed at Louis. ". . . So much as a matter brought about by the personal ambitions and the colossal vanity of the man on trial!"

A murmur of agreement passed among the spectators. Louis looked, to study the faces of the jurors.

The judge turned to Lemieux. "And how do you plead for the Defence?"

Lemieux rose, and turning slightly to face both judge and jury, said calmly, "Your Honour, we plead not guilty by reason of insanity."

The words hit Louis like a sledgehammer. He rose. "No! no! I will not permit this! They do not know me!" He turned backward where two of Lemieux's advisers sat. "These men are not from the West. They have . . ."

The judge brought down his gavel with a resounding bang, but Louis continued. "They have no grasp at all of what happened! I have discussed this with them . . ."

Again the judge's gavel hit the desk and his voice boomed through the courtroom. "Order! Sit down, Mr. Riel! If you do not like the way your counsel is dealing with your case, you may dismiss them and find new counsel, or conduct your defence yourself."

Louis sat down dejectedly. He turned to Lemieux. "I am not insane. I must speak, I must say what I have to say. I have much to say and there is little time."

Lemieux nodded and touched the hand of his client. "Let me do this my way. I promise you, you will have your moment."

Louis looked at Lemieux. He did not trust him. "You promise I will have an opportunity to . . ."

"Yes," Lemieux said, "we'll discuss this further when court is adjourned for the day."

Louis sat back in his chair and covered his ears to blot out the sounds, the people, everything. After a time he went back to his writing.

The cell was tiny and built with grey stones. It was not until Father McWilliams lit the single candle that Louis remembered his recurring dream. The stones, the candle, the voices, and the smell of burning flesh. He shivered and pulled the blanket from the cot and covered his legs and arms.

McWilliams looked at him. "Cold?"

Louis nodded. "Yes, yes, I am cold."

"It is damp in here. Louis, I must talk to you."

Louis' eyes fixed on the candle and on his unformed dream.

McWilliams' voice seemed somehow distant. "You have always responded before, Louis. Always. I want you to respond now. You must co-operate and hold your own words until the time is right." Louis nodded. The candle, the stones, the voices.

"When the time is right you will say the right things, Louis. You know what to say."

Louis nodded his head. "Yes," he muttered, "I will know what to say, I have it all planned."

"If you won't co-operate, he can't defend you."

"There are things that must be said." Louis' voice was stronger now, but McWilliams continued. "The prosecution has some signed statements from Métis who are pointing to you as the single driving force behind the rebellion. You must follow Lemieux's advice."

Louis put his hands to his temples. "What a ridiculous choice. If I'm innocent, it's because I am insane. If I'm guilty, I must die."

McWilliams put his arm around his old seminary friend. "You remember our history classes, Louis?"

Louis looked up at him. "Of course."

"You remember that Galileo was tried by the Pope for heresy. He chose to recant his theories and lived to be remembered for his genius. There was no shame."

Louis smiled at McWilliams. "And what about Sir Thomas More?"

"A man of great principle. He chose to die, and we remember his death, not his life."

Louis answered as McWilliams knew he would. "Galileo was not put in an asylum."

Louis continued to take notes and to prepare himself. Witness after witness came forward to prove him either insane or a murderer. He constantly badgered Lemieux with questions and counterarguments.

"For God's sake, Riel. It's time for the summation. Do not put words into my mouth!"

Louis grabbed Lemieux's arm and spoke loud enough for most of the courtroom to hear. "You have put them in mine; I am not insane!"

The judged banged his gavel and motioned to Lemieux, who rose, shaking off Louis' grasp.

"Your Honour, throughout this trial the defendant has been unco-operative and is now insisting on delivering his own summation."

The judge looked at Louis. "Mr. Riel, is this true?"

Louis stood calmly. "It is, Your Honour."

The judge peered down at him. "And do you realize the possible consequences of disposing with the defence of your learned counsel?"

"I do, Your Honour."

The judge shook his head in disapproval. "Then proceed," he said.

Louis stood and faced the blank faces of the jury.

"For many days now I have observed this trial conducted in a way that has neglected the true issues and left me no options."

Louis turned about and faced one of the witnesses, Father Ritchot. "On the stand, Father Ritchot has said that I took advantage of the ignorance of the Métis to make myself appear as a prophet to them. In fact, the Métis turned to me because the Catholic church watched them suffer neglect from our government for years and told them only to wait and be patient. It is hard to be patient when night after night you go to bed with your belly aching from starvation, watching your children die."

Louis leaned back against the table for a moment to catch his breath. Father Ritchot was pale and shaking and Louis knew he felt the stinging truth of the words directed at him.

Louis turned next to Charles Nolin, who sat impassively.

"Charles Nolin, the Métis 'representative,' has twisted everything I have done to make it appear selfish and evil. He claims that I conspired to return to the Saskatchewan seeking vengeance against the Canadian government for my exile."

Nolin's face did not change, but Riel continued his attack. "I was asked to return by the people of Batoche to try to convince the government to fulfill the promises it had made—a job that Charles Nolin was supposed to do but would not, for fear of jeopardizing his business contracts with that same government!"

Louis then turned to the ageing Dr. Roy, who leaned forward listening intently to his words. "On this stand, Dr. Roy has called me a megalomaniac, stating that I have a recurring mental disorder that has caused me to act as I have."

Louis turned back to the jury. "It is easier for them to call me a madman or a devil than to face the truth . . . and the truth is that when a government, over many years, continually misunderstands and mistreats a part of its people, it should not be surprised when those people speak out. And when that government turns a deaf ear to the pleas of those people, who are asking no more than what is their own right, that they be permitted to live as they wish, then that government should not be surprised when they rise up against it. The Métis are not birds of the air. We cannot live the way we once did, roaming the plains, following the buffalo. We need a place to light, a place to call our own and to belong, the right to maintain and develop our own identity and culture. And this has been denied . . . Yes, Dr. Roy, I still believe I have a holy mission. I dream that we can create a place of God in this huge country. A place where the oppressed peoples of the world could come, people who need this land . . . people who would love it and who would live in peace with themselves and with their God. Is that so different from what you believe? And yet I stand before you today not

196

only asking for my life, but asking you if this is the behaviour of an irrational man.

"I have watched my people die. I have seen an entire way of life trampled by a new civilization they did not understand. For a brief moment I stood in the path of this civilization, this progress . . . not to stop it, but rather to address the government, a government far away in the east, which had no idea of how my people lived or who they were. All I asked was respect for the rights and the dignity of the Métis. If this be madness, then I am mad! But I am in good company. If it be treason, then indeed I am guilty, for in this I will always believe!"

Louis leaned back, breathless and weary from his long speech, but thoroughly at peace with himself. He saw the eyes of Father McWilliams fill with tears as he sank back in his chair.

McWilliams watched the jury leave, terribly afraid what their verdict would be. He felt drained. All he could think of was Gabriel Dumont. He had once, many years before, asked Dumont if Louis was mad, and Dumont had replied, "If he is right, what does it matter?"

The judge looked at the faces of the members of the jury and asked Louis Riel to rise. "Gentlemen of the jury, have you reached a verdict?"

The foreman stood and grasped his paper. He looked at no one. "We have, Your Honour."

The room was totally silent. People held their breath and waited.

"May we have it?"

The foreman waited a moment and then blurted out the verdict: "We find the defendant, Louis Riel, guilty of treason!"

There were voices, shouting, the press leaving for the telegraph office. Louis closed his eyes and leaned on the prisoner's dock. "Guilty." The word rang in his ears . . . He was not insane after all.

The judge banged his gavel, demanding order, and in a few minutes the courtroom was silent again. "Louis Riel, this court has found you guilty, and I have only one more duty to perform. That is to advise you to meet your end. It is the sentence of this court that you be taken from here to the Police Guardroom at Regina. And that you be kept there until the eighteenth of September next, whence you shall be taken to the place appointed for your execution, and there hanged by the neck until you are dead. May God have mercy on your soul."

"Pray with me, Louis." Father McWilliams' voice was soft and distant.

"Are you afraid, Charles?" Louis looked into the warm, wet eyes of his friend.

"I am afraid for you, Louis."

"There is no need, my friend, no need. You have played out your role and I mine."

"I have not enjoyed the play, nor the role," McWilliams answered.

"Have you heard of Gabriel? Is he free as he must be?"

Father McWilliams nodded. "He is in the United States. He wanted to try to rescue you. He has tried everything."

"I am glad he failed. I am not to be rescued or denied my death."

McWilliams took Louis' hand. "No man is denied his death, only the moment of his death."

Louis looked into McWilliams' eyes again. "This is the moment I have chosen, Charles. You must not grieve. Please, pray only for my soul."

"Always," McWilliams replied. "Let us pray together." Together the two men knelt on the stone floor.

The door opened. The guard hesitated and then said simply, "It is time."

Silently they moved together out into the mid-November daylight. The sky was a deep blue, the air crisp and clean. The sun was only just rising in the distance. The birds that nested in the eaves around the courtyard twittered their early-morning chatter. The scaffold rose above them, the morning light casting long, strange shadows over the Métis people below.

Louis smiled at Father McWilliams. "It is a good day for a journey."

McWilliams tried to erase the pain from his face as they approached the scaffold, climbing the steps one by one.

Louis stood quite still. They tied his arms and placed the noose around his neck. Tears streamed down his friends' faces as the hangman placed the hood over Louis' head. "I have prayed for you, Charles. Courage, Father."

McWilliams summoned his last bit of strength. "Let us pray together. Our Father Who art in heaven, hallowed be Thy name . . . Thy kingdom come, Thy will be done, on earth as it is . . ." The trap door was pulled. Father McWilliams stopped in mid-sentence and opened his eyes. Louis' body was swinging from the rope. It seemed like an eternity.

McWilliams looked up at the sun now coming into view.

"Oh Louis," he said aloud. "Were you mad or sane? Were you a saint, a sinner? Were you a rebel as they said—or a patriot?"

No one heard his questions, but it did not matter anyway.

They were questions no man could answer.

Epilogue

Go play with the towns you have built of blocks,
The towns where you would have bound me!
I sleep in my earth like a tired fox,
And my buffalo have found me.

Stephen Vincent Benet

Gabriel Dumont escaped across the U.S. border and became a political refugee. For many months he tried to plan a daring escape for his close friend and companion, Louis Riel. None of his plans came to fruition and in the end he suffered much guilt over Riel's execution. He travelled the eastern seaboard addressing various French-speaking groups, and at one point even had an audience with the President of the United States. After a time he joined Buffalo Bill Cody's Wild West Show, where he met and performed with Sitting Buffalo, more commonly known as Sitting Bull.

In 1886 the Canadian government declared a general amnesty for the Batoche rebels, but distrustful of the government, Dumont did not return to Canada for several years. When he did come home, he settled on land he had originally claimed, land to which he was eventually given title. He built another cabin for himself near Batoche and often visited Duck Lake, the site of his most decisive military victory.

Gabriel Dumont lived out the rest of his life in good health. He fished and hunted often, was never ill, and remained active and vigorous.

On or about May 15, 1906, Dumont returned from a hunting trip. A few days later he went for a long walk in and around Batoche and stopped at the home of a relative. They talked and had a bowl of soup together. Dumont left the table, went to a nearby bed, and simply lay down and died.

Marguerite Riel died six months after her husband was executed. Always a frail woman, she died of consumption. Madeleine Dumont died in November, 1885, a few months before Marguerite Riel. She too appears to have died of consumption.

Donald Smith drove the last spike in the Canadian Pacific Railway on November 7, 1885. He became Canada's High Commissioner in London, was knighted in 1897, and died at the age of ninety-four on the eve of World War I.

Sir John A. Macdonald succeeded in uniting the country by rail, *a mari usque ad mare*, and successfully fought his last political battle in the election of 1891. He died three months later.

Bishop Ignace Bourget solidified his leadership of the Ultramontanist movement, which unfortunately succeeded in dividing the church in Quebec for a number of years.

Poundmaker and Big Bear were tried for their part in the 1885 rebellion, served three years of their sentence, and were released in 1887. Both died shortly thereafter.

Wandering Spirit, war chief of the Cree, was hanged, and he went to his death humming a love song to his wife.

Major L. N. F. Crozier resigned from the North West Mounted Police and visited Gabriel Dumont in New York.

It should perhaps be noted that Louis Riel's "mad" plan to open the West for settlement to the oppressed people of the world was at least partially adopted by the Canadian government ten years after his death, when immigrants were recruited from eastern and central Europe. The government, in 1971, also adopted Riel's suggested multicultural policy within a bilingual framework. And last but not least, a number of Indian, Métis, and non-status Indian land claims are still outstanding in the courts of the land.

Visionary? Madman? In the words of Gabriel Dumont: "If he is right, what does it matter?"

BOOKS BY

BARRY BROADFOOT

TEN LOST YEARS 1929-1939
Memories of Canadians Who Survived the Depression
by Barry Broadfoot
The Depression—as all its survivors know—was a time
when unbelievable things happened regularly. This book
is a picture of greed and heroism, a grassroots story that
still affects Canadians today.

SIX WAR YEARS 1939-1945
Memories of Canadians at Home and Abroad
by Barry Broadfoot
"Six War Years . . . is gamy, frank and funny and captures
the spirit of the war years, the taste of combat, and the
interrelations of people living in a hothouse atmosphere
better than any book yet written about Canada's war."
——J. L. Granatstein.

THE PIONEER YEARS 1895-1914
Memories of Settlers Who Opened the West
by Barry Broadfoot
In this book the pioneers themselves remember the years
from 1895 to 1914 when the Canadian West took its
modern shape. Barry Broadfoot has again created an un-
forgettable oral history of one of Canada's most remarkable eras.

ORDER FORM

MAIL SERVICE DEPARTMENT
PAPERJACKS LTD.
330 STEELCASE ROAD
MARKHAM, ONTARIO
CANADA L3R 2M1

No. of copies	Order No.	Title	Price
_____	7737-7094-1	TEN LOST YEARS 1929-1939	$5.95 _____
_____	7737-7114-X	SIX WAR YEARS 1939-1945	5.95 _____
_____	7701-0060-0	THE PIONEER YEARS 1895-1914	5.95 _____

Please add handling charges: 25¢ for one book
50¢ for two or more books   _____

Please enclose cheque or money order.

We cannot be responsible for orders containing cash.

TOTAL _____

(Please print clearly)

NAME _____

ADDRESS _____

CITY _____

PROVINCE _____ CODE _____

BIOGRAPHIES FROM

PaperJacks

BUSH PILOT WITH A BRIEFCASE
by Ronald Keith

Grant McConachie founded and built our own Canadian Pacific Airlines. He started out as a bush pilot, and his life is one great happy-go-lucky adventure.

RENE LEVESQUE
by Jean Provencher, trans. by David Ellis

A well-researched, absorbing account of the life story of the dynamic, controversial premier of Quebec who, more than any other man, controls the future of Canadian unity.

BETHUNE
by Roderick Stewart

Norman Bethune is a legend. For millions of people he meant inspiration, healing, education, amusement, and finally, a heroic example. After four years of scrupulous research Roderick Stewart has gone beyond the legend to create an authoritative and impressive book on the Canadian doctor who became a hero in modern China.

ORDER FORM

MAIL SERVICE DEPARTMENT
PAPERJACKS LTD.
330 STEELCASE ROAD
MARKHAM, ONTARIO
CANADA L3R 2M1

No. of copies	Order No.	Title	Price
_____	7701-0076-7	BUSH PILOT WITH A BRIEFCASE	2.50_____
_____	7701-0020-1	RENE LEVESQUE	2.50_____
_____	7737-7125-5	BETHUNE	1.95_____

Please add handling charges: 25¢ for one book
                                        50¢ for two or more books   _____

Please enclose cheque or money order.

We cannot be responsible for orders containing cash.

                                                        TOTAL   _____

(Please print clearly)

NAME _____

ADDRESS _____

CITY _____

PROVINCE _____ CODE _____

PaperJacks

THE FABULOUS KELLEY
by Thomas P. Kelley

Meet the King of the Medicine Men, a man who could make you beg him to take your money. During his nearly fifty years in the "med" game, Doc Kelley learned every trick in the book and became a living legend. His story is a hilarious and fascinating true fantasy.

RAT RIVER TRAPPER
by Thomas P. Kelley

Who was the strange loner who roamed the wastes of the Yukon in the late 1920s with a smoking rifle in his hands? The eskimos called him "the man who steals gold from men's teeth," but to others he was Albert Johnson, the Mad Trapper.

RUN INDIAN RUN
by Thomas P. Kelley

In June, 1906, two of the toughest rogues in the British Columbia interior were found murdered the day after a drunken brawl near the frontier community of Hazelton. When Simon Gun-an-noot learned he would be charged with the killings, he took to the woods and eluded the police for thirteen years.

ORDER FORM

MAIL SERVICE DEPARTMENT
PAPERJACKS LTD.
330 STEELCASE ROAD
MARKHAM, ONTARIO
CANADA L3R 2M1

No. of copies	Order No.	Title	Price
_____	7737-7058-5	THE FABULOUS KELLEY	$1.95 _____
_____	7701-0089-9	RAT RIVER TRAPPER	1.95 _____
_____	7701-0090-2	RUN INDIAN RUN	1.95 _____

Please add handling charges: 25¢ for one book
50¢ for two or more books   _____

Please enclose cheque or money order.

We cannot be responsible for orders containing cash.

TOTAL   _____

(Please print clearly)

NAME _____

ADDRESS _____

CITY _____

PROVINCE _____ CODE _____